I0548418

Forgotten

and other
Heartless tales

Titles by Jaimey Grant

Connected Regencies:

Honor
Betrayal
Deception
Intrigue
Entangled (Spellbound)
Heartless
Redemption
Forgotten, and other Heartless tales

Short Stories:

My Lady Coward: An Episodic Regency Romance
The 11th Commandment: A Serial Regency in Ten Parts
Gertrude's Grace: A Short Regency ~~Romance~~...uh, Comedy
Assassin's Keeper / Survival in Unlocked: Ten "Key" Tales
Eliza's Epiphany in Whispered Beginnings
The Dragon's Birth (fantasy)

Forgotten

and other
Heartless tales

A Regency Romance Anthology

by

Jaimey Grant

TreasureLine Publishing

Forgotten
and other Heartless tales
A Regency Romance Anthology
by Jaimey Grant

E-book edition first published Feb 2014
Paperback edition first published Jan 2017
ISBN-13: 978-1-61752-184-3

Cover design by Laura J Miller
www.anauthorsart.com
Stock photos from
www.depositphotos.com
www.periodimages.com
Published by TreasureLine Publishing
www.treasurelinebooks.weebly.com

Table of Contents

Forgotten

*and other
Heartless tales*

Loyalty

*Her heart
belonged
to a dead man...*

Chapter One

The Season
London 1824

The dancers swirled by, dresses billowing out with each swift turn of the waltz. Ladies smiled, content with their partners, satisfied they were pleasing their parents with their actions. Gentlemen smirked, pleased with their conquests, satisfied they held the prize of the Season. The vibrant gowns of the duennas and widows mingled with the muted tones of the débutantes, creating a shimmering rainbow in the candlelight, accented with sparkling gems.

Lady Michaella Harcourt stood off to the side, blessedly alone for the nonce. She'd managed to escape her partners, after having managed to keep them from demanding every last dance on her card. She simply couldn't endure one more moment of fake smiles and condescension.

She watched the dancers, bitterness tugging at her heart. She witnessed one young girl fall in love with the man who held her, his own eyes so focused on the girl in his arms that Michaella knew the rest of the world ceased to exist for them.

Tears stung the back of Michaella's eyes. She knew that feeling, remembered the all-consuming joy to be had with a gentlemen who returned one's regard. The press of a hand, stolen glances, and the assurance that he would speak one day, making his feelings known to all, kept one holding on. And if one found oneself alone with one's love, for just a moment, a stolen kiss, a sweet, soul-consuming embrace might be all one had to hold onto, years later.

The crack in her heart deepened, sending a shaft of pain through her body. She stumbled back, disappearing behind the shrubbery that lined the grand ballroom. Her shaking legs threatened to send her to the floor.

How could the pain remain so fresh after so many years? She'd found a man she loved, one who'd adored her, made her feel safe and secure. She may not have been allowed to marry him, spend her life with him, but she'd still had much more than most young ladies.

Years later, her pain should be nonexistent, or at least manageable. Yet she could no longer see her sister, her beloved sister, the one with whom she'd never had secrets.

As time passed the pain did not lessen, as she was told it would. It only increased, bringing envy and bitterness with it.

She envied her sister's happiness. Leandra was married to the worst man in England, yet her happiness was visible for all to see. Her duke treated everyone with contempt, but for Leandra he was a different man. He loved her and her alone. He'd changed for her. He continued to change for her.

And it was that very man who'd arranged a marriage for Michaella, the sister he'd gained through marriage. He'd found a man he approved of to be her husband. The arrangements, the details, and the final agreement were all carried out through letters, hidden from Michaella's mother. The countess would not look kindly upon the duke for interfering.

Good manners demanded Michaella at least call on the duke, on her sister, assure them both of her good health and continued love for them. It was no fault of theirs that the one man she truly loved was gone.

A tear escaped. Brushing it angrily away, Michaella straightened. It was enough. She could no longer wallow in her misery. She had to move on, and her betrothal was just the thing. Perhaps babies would help her leave the past fully behind, allow her to grow, maybe even find the happiness she'd so briefly enjoyed with Gabriel.

Just the thought of him sent the pain coalescing through

her. How could life be so unfair?

"Steady, my lady," a voice whispered close to her ear, making her jump. "You would not want the tabbies catching sight of you in such a state."

A shiver snaked her spine at the low cadence of the voice, the slight roughness coating the words. Michaella turned her head to look at the speaker but could see nothing more than a dim shape lingering just beyond the small tree directly behind her. The leaves effectively blocked the man from her view. He leaned against the wall, from what she could tell. Lady Blakeley had certainly commandeered a generous amount of shrubbery to decorate her ball.

"Thank you for your concern, sir," she whispered, unsure what to say to such a personal comment and uneasy at her sudden desire to step closer to the man. "I am well, I assure you."

"Nonsense," he scoffed. "I haven't seen tears like that since my sister's wedding. You weep the same angry, miserable tears as she, but I see no bridegroom. Are you unwillingly betrothed then, dreaming of your melancholy future?"

Turning fully, hardly able to believe the audacity—the *perspicacity*—of the stranger, she snapped, "My future is no concern of yours, sir. Kindly refrain from making such personal comments."

He shrugged, the movement catching the tiny bit of light that managed to penetrate their hiding place. "I assumed you needed assistance. Forgive my mistake." He stepped forward, the movement jerky. No doubt he'd had a bit too much to drink. "I will find another wall to hold up, leaving you to weep in peace." His bow was curt, clearly indicating that she'd managed to insult him.

The gall of the man! He'd made improper comments to her! His actions were at fault, not hers. She should be the one insulted, not him!

"You are clearly foxed, sir, so I will forgive your impertinence," she intoned, tilting her chin up and giving him a glare that would have made her mother proud. "It would be best if we were to forget this conversation ever happened."

"I couldn't agree more, Lady Michaella."

Before she had time to be properly surprised by his knowledge of who she was, he took one halting step away from her, out of the concealing bushes. The myriad candles poured their light on him, showing her the face and form of the man she'd insulted. His dark hair and eyes sent a pang of memory through her, reminding her so much of Gabriel. But his sharp features and the unforgiving firmness to his lips were just the opposite. Still, he possessed a pleasing countenance, the kind of gentleman she'd normally have giggled over with her sister when they were young and awed by a pretty face. Dressed in the typical black evening clothes, he stood tall but slightly stooped as he leaned heavily on his cane.

Remorse struck her. "I am sorry, sir," she breathed, horrified at her accusation of drunkenness. She stepped forward, willing to assist him.

He jerked away. "Do not!" he snapped, his words carrying only to her ears. "I am well aware I am crippled. I do not need the reminder that I am an object of pity, even to a selfish, spoiled brat such as yourself."

She recoiled, shocked at his unflattering summation of her character. She'd always been the quiet one, the quintessential lady, the calming presence in a volatile situation. No one had ever called her spoiled or selfish. No one ever insulted her the way this man did. She'd only been praised for her ladylike manners, protected from the cruel ugliness of life. Even when her sister married the duke and threat after threat landed at their feet, Michaella was still protected from the worst of it.

Culling all those old emotions from her deepest self, Michaella offered him a slight curtsy, enough to be polite without being insulting. She had no idea who this man was or how he ranked in Society. She refused to let him upset her. Besides, she was soon to be married, and she could leave Society far behind, content to live the rest of her life amongst her babies on some country estate.

"Regardless of what you think of me," she informed him with a tilt of her chin, "I do apologize for my words. I was wrong to make assumptions. I beg your forgiveness."

He stared at her, as if trying to determine if she played

him for a fool. Then, with a dignified nod, he capitulated. Three halting steps brought him back to her side. The shadows hid his features again but Michaella didn't need the light to see him. For some unfathomable reason, her mind recalled every aspect, right down to the tiny scar on his chin.

He took her hand. Michaella stared down at their gloved fingers, frozen in shock at the electric tingle emanating from the contact. How could she feel such raw, overwhelming awareness of a man she didn't even know? There was never this unsettling uncertainty with Gabriel, this sudden desire to disgrace herself with some unseemly behavior. And she'd loved Gabriel. Who was this mysterious man whose touch made her wonder if she'd lost her wits?

"I accept your apology and offer my own," he told her, his voice recalling her to the present and the very living, very real man before her. "My comments, though well-meaning, were personal, thus improper." He bowed over her hand, deeper than was warranted in light of her status, but she could detect no mockery in his action. "I bid you good eve, Lady Michaella." He pressed a kiss to her fingers, seemingly unaware of the soul-stealing breathlessness that assailed her.

She watched him leave, heart hammering against her ribs, confused and intrigued.

Unwilling to spare another thought for him, she forced

her mind and body to recall where she was, and how important it was for her to maintain the perfect composure, the perfect façade. She stepped from her hiding place on legs that almost refused to obey, her eyes searching the crowded room for her mother's commanding form. Seeing the countess deep in conversation with an equally forbidding matron—Lady Helmsley, if Michaella recalled correctly—she glanced back to her hiding place, longing to return there.

She'd had enough of the ball, and parties in general. Coming to a decision as unlike her as any decision could be, she neglected to bid her hostess goodbye and slipped out the French doors to her right.

Chapter Two

The following afternoon brought with it the gentlemen Michaella had danced with the previous evening. A night of fitful slumber had restored her equilibrium a trifle, though nothing could erase the humiliation she'd brought upon herself. She didn't even know the gentleman she'd insulted. She wondered if she'd ever see him again.

The odd thought occurred to her that she'd not formally met the gentlemen and what a shame that was. He certainly was pleasing to the eye and if they'd have been properly introduced, she would have found him very interesting indeed. As it was, she was having a hard time not thinking of him, wondering who he was and what had prompted him to speak to her at all. Her tears were certainly no problem of his and his willingness to inquire into her state of mind, though improperly forward, showed a caring nature.

Any thoughts of the strange reaction she'd had to his impersonal touch was firmly pushed aside.

It mattered little. She'd soon marry and would no longer have to fret over insulting strange gentlemen who accosted her in the shrubbery. Her lips twitched at the image she'd conjured.

Michaella smiled and conversed with the ease she'd long enjoyed, allowing her natural mildness to take over. She had no knowledge of half the things the ladies and gentlemen said, her entire being concentrated on saying and doing only what was proper, what was expected of a lady of her standing.

Leaving the ball the previous evening had been far easier than she'd anticipated. She'd simply sent a servant round for the carriage and to inform her mother of her departure. There was no objection because Michaella didn't linger to hear one. The lecture she'd received upon her mother's return an hour later was enough objection for anyone.

Why was she even attending the Season? At four and twenty, Michaella was so long on the shelf she'd begun gathering dust. Yet her mother insisted this one last time, one last attempt to marry her off to some obliging gentleman who didn't require her love. Love was the one thing she couldn't give.

She'd yet to inform her mother of her betrothal, knowing how much that woman would hate the Duke of

Derringer's interference. So for her mother, she pretended to enjoy the Season, unentangled, free to dance, flirt, and make merry.

A sigh rose up, escaping before she could counter it. Her companion stopped talking, his mouth hanging open in a ludicrous display of shock.

"I do apologize, my lord. You were saying?" she forced past her lips, her tone soothing despite her desire to escape the room. She settled more comfortably in her uncomfortable chair, determined to pay closer attention the man. It was no fault of his where her heart or her attention might lie.

"I believe Lord Melrose asked if you care for the cut of his coat? It is all the crack," offered a helpful voice at her other elbow.

Michaella's heart sank. "Sir? I am surprised to see you here. We did not dance." Her tone was less than welcoming, something Michaella was shocked to hear. Was she destined to always insult this particular man?

How could she not when his very presence incited some strange reaction in her, nervous anticipation mixed with dread? She didn't know what to expect in his company and she despised that.

His dark brows rose. "We did not, my lady, though I was unaware it was a prerequisite of paying a call on a charming lady." He glanced meaningfully at the chair on her other side, clearly wishful of sitting next to her.

In light of his infirmity, she could think of nothing more to do than nod, biting her tongue on the desire to ask him to leave. The sensations he caused were not normal and highly improper.

"It is not a prerequisite, sir, but a formal introduction certainly is," Michaella murmured.

His answering smile, the slight quirk of just one corner of his lips, sent a shock through her. He settled himself at her side, propping his cane against his leg. Her face heated as she realized just how rude she'd been to mention dancing when it was quite clear that he could do no such thing. What had come over her?

"Is it not fifteen minutes since your arrival, my lord?" the gentleman asked the man at her other side.

Young Lord Melrose shot to his feet, face reddening as he sputtered out an apology. "Your pardon, my lady. I quite lost track of the time. Your servant, my lady!" He snapped a very proper bow, leaving her side to offer his goodbyes to her mother.

Michaella watched him go, part of her regretting the loss of his company. He presented a harmless appearance, his manner nothing but kind, gentle, and lacking any cause for undue emotions. Her gaze slid to her new companion, heart stuttering at the sight of his dark blue eyes fixed firmly on her face. She pressed her hands together, alarmed at the sudden moisture between her palms.

"Now that we are alone—"

Michaella's eyes shot wide, then narrowed. She ignored the sudden pounding of her heart at the idea of being alone with him. "Hardly alone, sir! We are in a room full of people, any of whom will rush to my side at the mere crook of a finger." Her chin shot up, an affectation that was becoming more and more a part of her. When did she turn into such a harpy?

He chuckled. "Have you considered, my dear, that you have the power to have me removed? We have not been introduced, after all. Our conversing at all is most improper."

His dark eyes speared hers, daring her to do just as he proposed, have him tossed from her mother's home. She was tempted to do just that but remembered in time that she was a lady, a lady her father had been proud of, one he'd be ashamed to acknowledge after her recent behavior. Whatever reactions this man caused in her, she would not disgrace her father's memory with such a shocking display of bad manners.

"I would never behave in such a rude manner, sir, even if your behavior is less than polite," she countered. "And I apologize for my treatment of you. It was ill done of me."

He leaned away from her, a smile on his lips and in his eyes. "I do not believe you, Lady Michaella. Your eyes do not lie and in them I see your desire to have me thrown bodily from your home."

She smiled, despite her desire to be shocked. "My sister

would be deeply surprised at my behavior towards you," she told him, her eyes sweeping the room before she lowered her voice to add, "Truth be told, I am surprised at myself. I think your first words to me were too personal, too...true, for my comfort."

"Ah," he murmured. "You do face an unwelcome alliance. Who forces your hand? Your mother?"

"Nothing of the sort, I assure you," Michaella quickly inserted. "I was...merely unwell. But I am better now, I assure you."

Seemingly satisfied with her excuse, he settled in his chair, back straight and eyes serious. "I meant no insult. I did not care to see you so distressed, and knowing Society the way I do, they would be all too eager to serve you up as the latest *on dit*. Please forgive my impertinence."

There was a certain note in his voice, a particular inflection, that led Michaella to believe that he had firsthand experience with Society's willingness to pillory a reputation. Ashamed at her actions, though a direct result of his words to her, she covered his hand with her own, little regard for the forward manner in which she was behaving. What in her manner with this gentleman had been particularly proper anyway?

His muscles tensed, sending a shaft of heat through her gloved fingertips, but she didn't pull away. Dampening the sensation, she forced out, "I am sorry..."

Her pause prompted him to supply his name. Finally.

He stood, leaning heavily on his cane. "I have overstayed my welcome," he informed her, a blatant falsehood in light of the fact that he'd only been there all of five minutes, "so I will say my farewells. I bid you adieu, Lady Michaella."

She was not allowed to say anything. For a man with less than full use of one of his lower limbs, he moved very quickly! He was gone before her brain formed a single coherent thought.

Chapter Three

"You met her, then?" Derringer asked, his eyes locked on his guest's face. "Does she like you?"

Rhys Wainwright laughed, remembering the way Michaella's honeyed eyes flashed when he angered her. "No, I don't think she does, and I think that vexes her." He grinned at the duke, leaning back and sipping his brandy. "I have spoken with the chit all of ten minutes and managed to bring out her saucy side."

Derringer stared. "Michaella has a saucy side?" He tipped his head to his wife where she sat in one corner of the study silently stitching on an infant's gown. "Were you aware of this, my better half?"

Lady Derringer's eyes settled on Rhys' face. He wasn't sure what she sought in his gaze but his brows lifted of their own accord as her stare lengthened. Finally, she turned to glance at her husband.

"I have never known my sister to speak rudely, nor acknowledge a man to whom she has not been properly introduced." She smiled at Rhys. "I am encouraged by her behavior towards you, sir." And she returned to her sewing.

Rhys' gaze swept from one to the other, finally settling on Derringer's unsmiling countenance. "I have your approval, then?"

"You always did," the duke revealed, pouring a stiff measure of brandy into his glass and offering more to Rhys. "Michaella, however, had the power to reject you all along."

"Why didn't she? I did not behave well and the first time I saw her she wept bitter tears. It does not bode well for us if her tears were because of this betrothal."

And he didn't care for just how helpless he'd felt in the face of her distress. His protective instincts had risen to the fore, urging him to comfort her, draw her into his arms and reassure her that marriage to him would not be so bad. Instead, he'd insulted her with personal comments.

"Her tears have nothing to do with any betrothal," Derringer assured him. He tossed back the contents of his glass, almost as if he needed the temporary courage liquor could provide. "Truth be told, her heart lies with my brother."

That wasn't what Rhys had expected to hear. He didn't

care for the way his lungs stopped drawing breath, as if the thought of her in love with another man meant anything at all to him.

Rhys mentally shook himself and frowned. "Then why —?"

"Gabe is dead. She needs to move on, as the rest of us have."

Lady Derringer glanced up, lines of concern feathering her brow as she regarded her husband. "We miss him, to be sure, and always will," she assured Rhys, her gaze turning to him, "but my lord is correct. Michaella needs to leave the past in the past. She has always desired marriage and babies. She deserves love. And we agree that you can give her all that."

Rhys could hardly believe his ears. While the idea of making babies with the lovely Lady Michaella was decidedly...arousing, his mind balked at the idea of falling in love.

"Love? I do not know her. How can you be so sure love is possible? For her or me?"

"Are you so convinced it is not?"

Lady Derringer's question echoed in Rhys' brain. Was he sure? He'd loved once, a quiet, meek, biddable girl, a girl he'd known his whole life and who had still agreed to marry him even after a war injury left him crippled. Had she still loved him, broken man that he was? He supposed she had, in her way. No children had ever come of their union. She conceived once, delivered a stillborn son, and a year later she'd died, a thin, sickly shadow of the woman she'd once been.

He could not deny his desire for children, dozens of the little imps, if he could find a bride willing to bear them. He glanced at Lady Derringer, her eyes still on him but her hands tightly clenched in the garment she painstakingly trimmed with green ribbon. Would Lady Michaella be like her sister, content to sew clothing for her child, eagerly anticipating the child's arrival? Or would she, like many others in her position, resentfully bear only what her husband expected of her, the required heir and a spare?

"If Lady Michaella is content to marry a man she does not know in an effort to move on with her life, I am willing to prove to her that she made the best choice."

"Oh, lovely," breathed Lady Derringer, a delighted smile pushing up her plump cheeks.

"I may have to call you out, Wainwright," the duke grumbled. "You can't spout such romantic drivel within a woman's hearing and expect her husband to live in peace. Bloody hell."

The duchess smiled at her husband, murmured, "Language, love," and returned her attention to her sewing. Rhys sensed the lack of conviction in Derringer's tone but he knew the duke well enough by now to realize there existed the slightest chance of the threat coming to pass.

Just to be safe, he told the duke, "It won't happen

again."

As he rose to leave, he remembered the other reason he'd come. Reaching into his jacket pocket, he retrieved a small box. "If you would please present this to Lady Michaella, with my compliments."

Leandra smiled her agreement. Rhys bowed over her hand and departed, one part elated and one part defeated by the idea of his upcoming nuptials. However was he to make a woman forget the man she'd loved enough to mourn for nearly four years?

Chapter Four

Lady Michaella's visit to the Derringers was long overdue. The duke and duchess had gone to considerable trouble securing a suitable match for her, thus it behooved her to tender her gratitude in person. Shame filled her at the thought that she'd left it so long.

The duke's butler, a bull of a man who looked like the ex-pugilist he was, showed her to a room at the back of the house, bowing her in with no announcement. She smiled at him as he grunted something about tea and made his way back out.

"Bruiser!" The butler poked his head back in at the duke's call. "Fetch her grace."

The duke sat behind his desk, staring at Michaella, his harsh features appearing harsher than usual, a long thin scar adorning his face from his hairline to his chin. He still dressed entirely in black, from his straight black hair hanging loose over his shoulders to black linen. She assumed what she couldn't see of him was clothed in black as well. He'd forgone a coat, lounging in shirtsleeves, something Michaella wasn't used to but had learned to ignore years ago when she'd spent much time in the duke's presence.

And just seeing him now, after all these years, brought a pang of longing to her heart so strong that she thought she might come over faint. He was a mirror image of his brother, if one discounted the scar and the overly long hair. But her reaction should not be so strong. Derringer's face had a hardness that Gabriel's lacked. That simple reminder restored her equilibrium.

"Lady Michaella, what brings you to my humble abode?" He didn't stand, a circumstance unsurprising to Michaella. Good manners weren't his strength and never had been.

"I am come to thank you, Hart." She strode further in, removing her gloves as she did so. Glancing around, she spied a small table next to a chair. "May I?"

Derringer grunted, showing no remorse for his rudeness.

Michaella smiled fully. "I have missed you," she said, tossing her gloves on the table and removing her bonnet. He smiled at her in response, the sudden change in his expression causing a brief flutter in her middle. Now he more closely resembled his twin, so much it hurt.

"How fares my sister? Vexed with me, I don't doubt." Her heart hurt at the idea but she attempted a light tone. If things took on too serious a note during her visit, she would cry and that she couldn't allow.

Derringer's smile vanished, replaced with a dark scowl. He tipped his head to the door. "Ask her yourself."

"Darling, your manners," chastised a new voice, lighter, feminine.

Michaella turned to the door, ignoring the duke's answering grunt. She did note, however, that he went to the effort of rising from his seat, a show of respect he seemed to reserve only for his wife. A spurt of envy shot through her at the thought of a man changing himself for the woman he loved, of a love so strong that a person would want to change. And her sister had changed too, choosing to understand the background behind the duke's bad behavior rather than eradicate it from him. Leandra had never once believed all the change should come from one half of the relationship. How Michaella wanted what they had!

"Merri, how I've missed you." Michaella couldn't prevent the tears that trembled on the greeting. Her sister had been her dearest friend at one time. Just saying her name aloud, the name Leandra had preferred as it was a pet name given to her by their father, filled her eyes with moisture.

"Oh, dearest Kaylee, how good it is to hear that name on your lips once again. I'd begun to despair of ever seeing you again!" Leandra's eyes glistened suspiciously and she pulled a handkerchief from the long sleeve of her sapphire blue velvet gown. Wiping away the offending moisture before it could make tracks down her pale cheeks, she then stuffed the scrap back into her sleeve.

A moment later the women embraced, showing far more emotion than Society ladies ought. Michaella savored the moment, not having realized until that instant just how alone she'd felt in the past three years.

"Merri, my love, I will leave you ladies and see what Bruiser has done with the tea." Derringer bowed in their general direction, but the ladies ignored him.

Tears caused few good reactions in gentlemen. Michaella wondered how her soon-to-be husband would react. Gabriel had held her when she'd cried, but in the years since his death she'd learned to stem the flow before it started. She'd learned to change much about herself over the years. Very little of the meek, quiet, content girl remained. At least, in her own mind. Outwardly, she was as mild as ever.

Except when she was with a certain gentleman. She determinedly shook that thought away.

"I am so pleased to see you," the duchess said, seating herself next to Michaella's chair. "What brought about this surprise visit?"

"I thought it time to thank you and Hart for arranging a marriage for me. It was very kind of you to take such an interest in my happiness."

Leandra settled deeper in her chair, hands clasped in her lap. "It was our pleasure, my dear, but you have no need to thank us. I just hope we have chosen well and that you find some peace with Mr. Wainwright."

Michaella couldn't prevent a sigh. "I will try my best, Merri, but I cannot promise to love him. You are sure he is well aware of that? I would not want to mislead him into thinking this could ever be a love match."

Leandra smiled, reaching over to pat her hand. "He is prepared to start a life with you and allow fate to take control."

"A pretty sentiment," Michaella mused. She nodded. "I can be of the same mindset as Mr. Wainwright. I will marry him, fully intending to be content in my decision."

"Oh! I have something for you," Leandra informed her then, retrieving something from the duke's desk. "Mr. Wainwright left this for you." She placed a jeweler's box in Michaella's lap.

Surprised at the gesture, Michaella took it up, gazing at it in some wonder. She'd not expected such a thing, though it was not uncommon for a man to give his betrothed a gift.

Opening it, she frowned.

Leandra, seeing her sister's expression leaned forward. "What is it?"

Michaella lifted the necklace from its velvet bed, holding it up for Leandra's inspection. The duchess frowned right along with her. "It's black. What kind of gentleman gives his bride a mourning necklace?"

Leandra took it, turning it over in her hands, biting her lip as she did so. "Perhaps he meant something by it and will explain when you finally meet."

"Is it a jest, do you think?" A sudden, horrifying thought sucked the air from her lungs. "Does he know of Gabriel and mocks my pain?"

"He does know of Gabriel, but he would never mock you," Leandra affirmed. "Mr. Wainwright is the sweetest, gentlest man. He would never play a jest on you, especially one so cruel."

Michaella's lungs resumed their normal activity. "Of course not. I know you and Hart would never allow a trickster to take advantage."

She took the necklace back and really looked at it. Despite the oddity of a man giving his betrothed a necklace featuring a large black stone set in copper and suspended on heavy copper chain, it was a beautiful piece, expensive, too, if she wasn't mistaken. The midday sun streaming in through the window beside her lit the smooth black surface and brought little lights to the copper surrounding it.

"I am pleased you trust us so much in this, Kaylee."

Why did she? Why was she placing so much trust in her sister to secure her happiness instead of taking on the task herself?

Because she no longer trusted herself. She'd trusted her feelings once and suffered a hurt that even time couldn't heal. She was done with that kind of pain and determined that a peaceful union of mutual contentment and respect was of far more value than a love match fraught with emotion and the potential for heartache.

"I do. I have faith that this match will finally bring the peace and contentment I've always desired."

Leandra frowned. "Is that really all you want, dearest? A love match should not be regarded as undesirable. It is a completion of oneself, of one's very being. Please do not settle in this marriage as if love is not only an impossibility but unwanted. It is not fair to you or your intended."

"I have no intention of disallowing love," Michaella promptly soothed, brushing a finger over the smooth surface of the necklace she still held. She wouldn't have to disallow it. It quite simply wouldn't arise. Stifling a sigh, she tucked the bauble back into its box and stowed it in her reticule.

Thankfully, Bruiser chose that moment to deliver the tea. Leandra rose to attend to the task, smiling at the stocky man and saying something to him that elicited a return smile. Michaella watched this byplay, observed the ease with which Leandra conducted herself. She had few servants, a husband who eschewed Society and behaved in all manner of ways to cause any number of negative emotions, all while deflecting the rancor of those who even years later chose to despise her for her illegitimacy. And yet, the Duchess of Derringer thrived. Michaella admired her, envied her even.

Bruiser offered the ladies a clumsy bow and left. Leandra returned to her chair and poured tea for them both. Michaella watched, her eyes glued to her sister's face.

"How do you do it, Merri? How do you watch Hart take part in things that threaten his life, yet not go mad with worry?" She tried to keep her tone even, mildly inquiring, but didn't think she succeeded.

"Oh, love, I've come to accept that Hart will be Hart and I can either make myself miserable trying to change him or love him as he is. I've chosen to love him and trust that his love for me will temper his more reckless inclinations." Her smile was strained around the edges but determined nonetheless.

Michaella sighed and sipped her tea. "I don't suppose it's any different for any other match based on love. Give and take, change and acceptance, contentment and worry." She forced a smile, unwilling to admit, even to herself, that it sounded quite lovely to her. "It does give one a certain understanding of the wisdom of arranged matches based on mutual wealth and social consequence."

"Does it?" Leandra asked, eyebrows nearly touching her hairline in her surprise. "I never thought to hear such a sentiment from you, my dear. It saddens me to hear it."

Michaella had no reply and felt the slightest twinge of guilt at voicing such a thing. Of course she did not believe it. "However did we get on a subject so very dour? Let us change it."

"Very well." The duchess favored Michaella with a mischievous grin. "Have you informed your mother of your betrothal?"

Michaella's cup clattered alarmingly against her saucer. "I have not. Can you imagine the hysterics she would have? She has not forgiven Hart for marrying you, you know, even though she would normally forgive a duke for anything."

"Darling, Lady Harwood has not forgiven Hart for throwing her from his house."

They chuckled over the memory. Lady Harwood had never been so insulted in her life. At the time, Michaella had felt sorry for her, as she'd often felt sorry for others when they suffered. Now, some small, petty section of Michaella's heart rejoiced in her mother's humiliation.

Lady Michaella had changed over the years. Where once she'd had nothing but soft, kind words and ladylike manners, she now exhibited the occasional bout of cynicism and rudeness, her interaction with a certain gentleman topping any other moment.

"I suppose I shall leave you now," Michaella said after several moments of companionable silence.

"Must you? I haven't seen you for ages."

"I have things I must do before my wedding. There is but a fortnight before I become Mrs. Wainwright, you know."

"You can meet him before you promise to love and obey him, Kaylee," Leandra gently reminded her. "I think it would be for the best. I take no issue with you asking for an arranged marriage but to marry him sight unseen? Is that wise?"

"Your concern does you credit, Merri, but it is misplaced," Michaella assured her. "I am content waiting for the vows to see his face." She set her bonnet on her head and tied the ribbons, then reached for her gloves. "I trust his countenance is pleasing?"

"Oh my, yes," Leandra breathed, an almost dreamy quality transforming her plump features.

Michaella laughed. "Oh, Merri, my dear, are you smitten with my betrothed? What does your duke think of that?"

"He hates it," the man in question muttered as he strode purposefully back into the room. Rifling through some papers on his desk, he added, "He would run your betrothed through if the blighter hadn't agreed to marry you."

"What have I to do with it?" Michaella couldn't help asking.

The duke shot her an annoyed look, but refrained from commenting.

"Don't speak of yourself as though you are not in the room, dear," Leandra remonstrated. "It is hardly Rhys' fault that he is so pleasing to look upon and employs pretty manners too."

"If not his fault, then whose?" Derringer countered.

Leandra moved to her husband's side and laid a gentle hand on his arm. Smiling, she gazed up at him. "My love, you like Rhys or you would not have approached him about marrying Michaella. Refrain from any more of this false anger."

He growled but kissed the top of her head. "Next time he calls, you are not to see him. Pleasing countenance indeed. Bloody hell."

"Language, my love."

"You'd like to hear more?"

"I will leave you to battle this one without me," Michaella inserted before the duke could make good on his threat. "Thank you for the tea. I will be sure to call often in the coming weeks." She took her leave after a parting embrace from her sister and a surprising, affectionate squeeze from the duke. The man was a puzzle.

Chapter Five

"You are developing a deplorable habit of lurking in shrubbery."

Michaella turned, embarrassed and thankful for the darkness that hid her heated cheeks. "You catch me at the worst moments," she admitted with a short laugh. "What of you, Monsieur Pénombre? Do you often lounge in darkened corners?"

"I do." She could hear the laughter in his words. "Especially when hoping to catch a certain lady alone."

Michaella couldn't help the thrill that coursed through her at his words. She'd done the unthinkable in the past week, lingering in shadowed alcoves, behind lines of greenery, and in darkened corners, just hoping this particular man would appear.

Nothing this exciting had ever happened to her, not the pure thrill of being pursued by a gentleman who refused to share his name. She'd taken to calling him Monsieur Pénombre, because they always met in semi-darkness, though he wasn't French, that she could tell. It amused her to call him that, and it seemed to amuse him that she did.

This nameless gentleman teased her and flirted with her, making her forget, for a moment, Gabriel's laughing blue eyes and his smothering concern for her wellbeing. On that thought, she forced herself to speak, afraid she'd lapse into a melancholy at the idea of being disloyal to a dead man.

"What an improper thing to say, Monsieur. Do you often lay in wait to accost unattached ladies?"

Michaella's smile slowly disappeared as his silence wore on. Just when she thought he'd say nothing, he spoke, his voice deepened with some emotion she couldn't name.

"Are you, Lady Michaella?"

She shook her head, even though she didn't know if he could see her. "Am I what?"

He moved closer. She still couldn't see much of his features but his bearing told her he labored under some intense emotion. "Unattached."

Her heart stuttered. He couldn't know, it was impossible! "Yes," she blurted, terrified the truth would drive him away. Guilt stabbed her. How disloyal to her betrothed!

One more step and his booted feet brushed her green

skirts. "Yes, you are unattached or yes, you are attached?"

His breath whispered over her face, his nearness sending shivers along her spine. This was most improper, her position with this man, but she couldn't force her limbs to step away. She needed to step away, needed to run from his presence. Everything about her current situation was wrong.

"Does it matter?" she asked. "I am not married."

His gloved finger brushed her cheek. Michaella sucked in a breath. "You are not married yet, my lady. But you will marry."

"Someday. Perhaps." She wasn't lying, she reasoned, though she couldn't decide why she didn't just tell him of her betrothal. Did she harbor some secret doubt?

"Someday soon, no doubt." He withdrew, leaving her with the feeling that she'd been rejected.

Shaking the feeling aside, she asked, "Does that worry you? If you wait for me in alcoves why would you fret over such an inconsequential thing?" Though she knew how very important such a thing as a betrothal really was. A betrothal was a legally binding agreement. A jilt could find him or herself in a courtroom faced with a breach of contract suit.

"Inconsequential? You view the matter lightly, very lightly indeed." His tone held none of the warmth to which she'd become accustomed. She detected instead a tinge of disapproval in the rough cadence.

"What do you really intend to say, sir? You accost me and complain that I am here. What possible motive can you have for doing so if you worry over my mythical husband?" The worst possible thought occurred to her, sending her stumbling away from him. She stepped to the edge of the greenery, only stopping because she feared discovery. "You look only to ruin me?"

He chuckled. "Lady Michaella, I have no plans to ruin you. Your actions do not speak well for your own motives, however."

Before Michaella could form a response, he left her, vanishing into the shadows beyond her vision.

Chapter Six

"Do you have any dances free?"

Michaella's jaw dropped. "Sir?"

Rhys chuckled, his eyes sliding appreciatively over her upswept brown curls and classically beautiful face to settle briefly on the necklace she'd decided to wear with her uncommonly bright emerald green ball gown. He met her eyes again. "I asked for your dance card. Am I too late? Have you been secured for every one?"

Her eyes grew so wide he thought they'd surely burst. "What can you want with my dance card?"

"Really, Lady Michaella, the way you behave, one would think you had no knowledge of a dance card and how it works. Here, allow me to explain," he offered, twitching her card from her nerveless fingers and possessing himself of the seat beside her. He propped his cane against the back of the chair where it would be out of the way. "This is a dance card." He held it up for her inspection. "Each dance planned for the evening is listed and next to each is a blank line where a gentleman can sign his name should he wish to spend that dance with you."

She scowled, quite the most adorable expression he'd ever seen. "I am quite familiar with how a dance card works, Mr.—"

"You assume I am a mere mister? I'm insulted." How much could he tease her, he wondered, before she walked away or slapped him?

"I am merely pointing out our lack of introduction."

Her patience was wearing thin. He could hear it in her voice. Clearly, the clever little moniker she'd bestowed upon him was no longer amusing.

He took her little pencil and wrote his name in every blank slot on her card, some imp inside him laughing at his actions. Smiling, he handed it back to her and watched her slip the band around her wrist, her eyes never leaving his face.

Then she glanced at the card. Stunned golden eyes shot to his and narrowed into a glare. "Monsieur Pénombre?"

He smiled. "It's a very clever name, one I am quite honored to accept." He refused to tell her who he was and could only surmise she'd not asked someone else because she didn't partake in gossip. What an encouraging thing to learn about one's future wife. It was a rare lady indeed who didn't destroy reputations with the mere repetition of a hurtful bit of nonsense.

Her features could never look particularly threatening but Rhys saw the lines furrowing her brow and knew it was as angry an expression as she could muster. How long would he keep up such a charade? His smile widened into a grin. As long as he could. Why not let her get to know him while she could, let him get to know the real her, not the perfect lady the Derringers claimed she was? He could think of no better way to avoid the transformation from delightful termagant into pattern card Society débutante.

"I do not find this funny, sir," Michaella fumed. Her slender, gloved hands curled into fists in her lap.

"That I wish to dance with you? I assure you, I only intend to sit at your side and enjoy a conversation or two."

"It is most improper for me to spend this many dances in your company, even if we do not dance. It is tantamount to a proposal."

"And what, my dear girl, would be wrong with that?"

He hardly knew what made him say the words but there they were, like a breathing thing between them. Yet there was something in him that needed to know what she'd say.

She stared in open mouthed shock, her gaze traveling over him once to return to his face and linger there. He felt her gaze like a caress, brushing over his brow, his cheeks, his lips. Just when he thought he might actually blush under the force of her regard, she met his eyes.

"I am betrothed, sir, and not in the habit of engaging myself to gentlemen I do not know." Was it his imagination, or did he detect a note of longing in her voice?

"Indeed. And where is your affianced? Is he here?"

As her fingers came up to touch her necklace in an oddly nervous gesture, her gaze swept the room, not settling on any face or form. When she answered, a sigh floated on the words. "I do not know. I have never met him."

He couldn't help the chuckle that emerged. "So you are indeed in the habit of engaging yourself to gentlemen you do not know."

She turned fully, her knee brushing his. He felt a burst of flame where they touched but she seemed to experience nothing out of the ordinary, at least, nothing he could tell.

"It is a unique situation, sir, and not one I am prepared to discuss with you. As I've said, time and again, we have not even been introduced."

He leaned away, needing a moment of space between them. How could such a meek young woman have such an effect on his senses? It wasn't as though he craved a woman. He'd never been one to think women were only there for the use of a man, and he'd always believed a man could control his baser urges. So why, when everything hinged on him maintaining some distance, did this woman of all women inflame him?

"And yet you would marry a man to whom you have not

been introduced. Why?" And why did he insist on asking her such a thing?

"I fail to see how that concerns you," she retorted hotly, drawing herself up, her back so straight it reminded him of the backboard his mother used to make his sister wear to perfect her posture. "Furthermore, I fail to see what right you have to inquire."

Her gaze went over his right shoulder, a smile lighting her features in a way that could only be caused by a man. Rhys felt a surge of jealousy—of all things!—and glanced over his shoulder at an importuning young man some years his junior. The boy was barely out of leading strings. Lord Dunley, if Rhys remembered correctly.

"My dance, I think," the boy murmured, shooting a questioning glance at Rhys. To his credit, the boy didn't appear nervous, merely curious.

Rhys smiled. If the boy thought Rhys had some claim on Lady Michaella, that was all to the good.

Lady Michaella rose, forcing Rhys to rise as well. He scrambled up, reaching for his cane as he did so. When his hand came up empty, he stumbled, his body colliding with Lady Michaella. Her arms wrapped around him, a natural instinct, he was sure, one he could have done without. Just as naturally, his arm wrapped around her as well.

"Sir!"

He grinned. Her tone was part concern, part offense and he wasn't sure which was more adorable. Though he really could have lived without the humiliation of being unable to stand without the aid of his stick.

"My lady?"

"Must you hold me so tight?" she breathed, her voice so low he almost didn't catch the words.

His chuckle disturbed the tiny hairs caressing her brow. "I am not yet steady enough to release you," he prevaricated, unable to prevent his smile. How he'd once detested his awkward stumbling, his inability to move about in a normal fashion. Humiliation should have consumed him now but he could only revel in the feel of Michaella's lush form pressed against him.

The impropriety of their stance crashed over them when young Lord Dunley, who still waited patiently beside them, cleared his throat. "Mr. Wainwright, sir, do you need some assistance?" His low voice carried only to their ears, his desire not to embarrass anyone clear in his open, honest face.

Rhys' eyes slid shut, only to shoot open again when he found himself released from Michaella's grip. He teetered for only a moment. Dunley reached out and grasped his arm, reaching down to retrieve Rhys' cane and shove it into his hand. He nodded to the boy, part of him dreading the coming scene. What young lady, feeling she'd been tricked, wouldn't treat the trickster to a well-deserved harangue?

"Wainwright?" she said, face ghostly pale in the myriad flickering candles around them. Her fingers again touched the unusual necklace, the very bauble he'd given her. "Mr. Rhys Wainwright?"

He nodded. What else could he do, under the circumstances?

"You are... we are..."

Lady Michaella at a loss was unutterably sweet but his conscience stabbed him for causing it. "Yes, we are betrothed. Now, Lord Dunley has been waiting patiently this age and I think it best for you to enjoy his company."

Before either of them could protest, he kissed Lady Michaella's hand and walked away.

Chapter Seven

If Michaella had been one to hold a grudge, she had the perfect opportunity. What she felt was so far beyond such a mundane emotion that she refused to accept it. So in true Lady Michaella fashion, she donned her best ladylike manners, saying not one word against her future husband.

She also refused to say a word *to* her future husband, though less than one day remained before their wedding.

She kept her promise to Leandra, visiting every day before the wedding. She remained mum about discovering Mr. Wainwright's identity but every time the duchess brought up the subject of the man, Michaella refused to be drawn. She was not ready to discuss him, even with her sister.

The man was a disease in her blood. She'd seen him at a

gathering or two in the past few days and just the sight of him filled her with anger, curiosity, confusion, and longing. She'd enjoyed his company, not having experienced such entertainment since Gabriel. In fact, if she was truly honest with herself, her time with Gabriel had not been half so entertaining.

Rhys teased her mercilessly, disregarded propriety to see her reaction, made her smile at his antics, all treatment she'd not come to expect from gentlemen. Gentlemen flattered her for being the daughter of an earl, possessing a generous dowry, and because despite her age, even now, she would be a perfect wife. Lady Michaella Harcourt was a true lady, never flustered, never rattled, never crass or bold, never shrewish.

Until Mr. Rhys Wainwright.

What she could not understand was his seeming delight with her bad behavior. Why would a gentleman want a lady to step outside her training, reveal she was not the perfect lady?

"You seem far away."

Michaella started, her unfocused gaze settling on her mother. The woman's concern was odd, but Michaella chose not to mention that.

"I was thinking."

"Indeed? What about?" The countess didn't sound particularly interested but the fact she'd even asked meant she was.

About an infuriating man who prompted her to act without thought, say things she'd never even think let alone voice, and caused any number of improper thoughts.

And how guilt at her actions with a man she was not engaged to marry had prompted her to wear a necklace given to her by her betrothed, as a simple reminder to herself that she was not free.

None of these were things she could discuss with the Countess of Harwood.

"I was wondering about Father's will."

Lady Harwood's cup rattled against her saucer. Lips pinched, she looked her daughter straight in the eye and said, "I have it."

"What! All this time?" It was impossible! The duke handed the location of the will over to Lee in an effort to save Gabriel. But that meant...

"Derringer knew all along that you had it." Calm settled over her, but she wasn't sure how she really felt. If Hart had known, why hadn't he told his wife? Did any of that matter now, years later? Leandra was happy and didn't need the money their father left her. She had the locket she'd treasured and that was all that mattered to her. And Gabriel was dead. Nothing could change that.

Focusing again on her mother's face, she asked, "How could you have hidden that from Merri and Lee?"

"Your father saw fit to leave most of his fortune to that slut—"

"Mother! Merri is no such thing!"

Lady Harwood scowled. "Very well. He saw fit to leave most of the money to *her*, that girl he allowed to be named after him. I couldn't see his legitimate children so overlooked. Without the will, his son and heir inherited, as is only right."

"But Lee disappeared and was proclaimed dead, his firstborn son given the title and the money."

The countess leaned forward to pour more tea, taking a seed cake for herself and offering more to Michaella. The latter declined the cake, but accepted tea. Settling comfortably in her chair, back ramrod straight, feet neatly together, Lady Harwood proceeded to explain.

"Harwood is in France. He is well, has remarried, and is expecting another child come summer."

His first wife, Mirabel, died of a fever just after Michaella's brother disappeared. Her children were ensconced in the Harwood country estate, wreaking havoc.

"How can you know this? You have been in contact with him?"

"But of course," Lady Harwood tittered. "I am his mother. He would certainly inform me of his arrival."

"And how did you come by the will?"

"I told you, darling, I already had it. I've always had it. I knew where your father kept it and he never cared for lawyers. Uncivil creatures, he called them. I knew the will at home would be the only one in existence."

The smug superiority on the countess's face was reminiscent of years gone by, years Michaella thought long behind them. Seeing the return of the woman she'd known for so many years, the unloving, selfish, brutal woman who'd endured her husband's adultery by torturing the daughter he'd produced by another woman, Michaella's heart sank. Part of her had believed her mother had changed, finally accepting that no matter the late earl's actions, his daughter was not to blame.

But Michaella should have realized that Leandra's presence was a constant reminder of the earl's infidelity, a constant insult to a woman who'd prided herself on having made the perfect Society marriage. Thus the countess held Leandra accountable for her humiliation and when the moment came in which she could punish the girl once and for all, she'd stolen the will and tossed her out without a care for how she'd manage. It must have galled her to find Leandra had met and married a duke.

"Michaella? What ails you, girl?"

Michaella said nothing. She stared at her mother, thoughts in a whirl. The guilt over her betrothal dissipated, leaving a dull resignation in its wake.

"I am to be married, Mother. Tomorrow."

Lady Harwood's delicate china cup didn't merely rattle against the saucer this time. It shattered. "*What*?" Her question was a mere breath of sound, a horrified whisper.

Carefully setting her own cup and saucer aside,

Michaella rose and went to tug the bell pull. Not bothering to wait for a maid, she went to her mother's side and crouched down with her handkerchief, carefully cleaning up the glass and tea.

"Don't!" the other woman ordered, stopping Michaella's hands. "Tell me."

There was concern there, something Michaella hadn't ever thought to see in her mother's bearing. Her heart clenched at the sight. "I am betrothed, Mother. I have been for some weeks now."

"But— who? How?"

She'd never seen her mother at such a loss, not even when Derringer had thrown her from his home all those years ago. Reminding herself of what her mother had only just revealed—her hiding of the late earl's will—Michaella hardened her heart.

"He is Mr. Rhys Wainwright," she revealed, watching her mother's features closely. "The match was arranged by...a friend...over the course of several months. An agreement was reached, as I said, some weeks ago."

Lady Harwood froze, disentangling her hands from Michaella's. "Who?"

"I just told you—"

"No. Who arranged this?"

Michaella sat back on her heels. "Lord Derringer."

Lady Harwood's screech echoed off the rafters, finding every corner of the townhouse and shooting out into the streets. Surely it was heard by every resident of London.

Michaella slowly pushed to her feet. This was the mother Michaella had come to know, this harpy whose manners were reserved only for those who could hurt her socially, those whose opinions truly mattered not at all. Michaella had no power to ruin her.

But Derringer did and Lady Harwood despised him for that power, even though he'd never done anything to ruin her, never cared enough to think about her. Michaella understood her mother's hatred for the duke but her display of rage now was out of proportion to the situation. Derringer had done a great service finding a nice gentleman for Michaella to marry and her mother should be grateful.

The maid entered, took one look at the enraged countess, and promptly left. Michaella could only imagine what gossip would fly in the servants' quarters.

"Yes, Mother, Derringer found a husband for me, a nice man with a pleasing countenance and pretty manners. He will make me a good husband."

"Pretty manners? Pleasing countenance? These are the things you consider to be of importance in a marriage?"

Michaella felt the vitriol in each word. "Yes, these are the things that are important to me, Mother. And he owns property in the country so I can finally be free of London."

The countess eased back in her chair a bit. "Indeed?"

"Yes. He is not a poor man, Mother, but one with enough wealth to provide a comfortable home. I shall be happy."

This last she uttered as if trying to convince herself and perhaps she was. But some niggling thought in the back of her mind warned that her happiness would have a price. For moments of joy, she could experience indescribable misery.

Her eyes fluttered shut, a sudden realization almost making her faint. It was impossible to care on such short acquaintance, yet Michaella found herself caring very much where Mr. Rhys Wainwright was concerned.

Not even bothering to beg her mother's pardon, Michaella left the room. She needed to call on her sister immediately.

Chapter Eight

Rhys learned a lot about his bride in the days she refused to entertain him. Her manners were beyond reproach. She treated him with the same polite propriety as she did any other gentleman. It was infuriating!

Rhys was a proper gentleman, to be sure, but he was quickly reaching his breaking point. She didn't call off their engagement, the date advancing with alarming speed, but she didn't make an effort to get to know him before the day either. And if there was one thing Rhys wanted from his future wife, it was a willingness to become better acquainted.

The day before the wedding that had yet to be called off, he called on the Derringers. He'd never been one to lose his temper but he was dangerously close now. He'd developed feelings for Lady Michaella that he hadn't anticipated, realizing he was unwilling to allow her to just accept him. She had to *want* to marry him.

Maneuvering his way up the front steps of Derringer's townhouse, Rhys could hardly comprehend the frustration consuming him. He'd given her a week to come to terms with their future and she'd done nothing that he could tell in order to do so.

The duke's bullish butler bowed him in, not even bothering to announce him. He merely opened the drawing room door and backed away, disappearing into the nether regions of the house.

Rhys shrugged. He'd met his share of eccentric servants in his time. Bruiser wasn't the first ex-pugilist Rhys had met and certainly not the first to find employment in the household of a prominent peer. And if even a fraction of the things Rhys had heard about Derringer were correct, the duke was in more need of a trained fighter than most.

The drawing room stood empty. Rhys meandered over to the hearth, his gaze sliding over feminine knickknacks, Dresden shepherdesses frolicking with their sheep while ridiculous little crystal ducks gazed on in empty absorption. Such an incongruous sight in the duke's abode.

The click of the door snagged his attention. He stared at the arrival, a slow smile curving his lips.

"Lady Michaella," he greeted, his eyes traveling over her smart walking ensemble. She no longer wore the pastels of a débutante, choosing instead to wear the bolder colors of a matron. Perhaps she felt her age entitled her to such a choice. The necklace he'd bestowed upon her was conspicuously absent.

Her lovely features pulled into a frown. "Mr. Wainwright."

He approached, leaning heavily on his cane. "I know I angered you with my charade but I promise I did not set out to deceive you."

"Did you not?" she asked, pulling her bonnet strings and tugging the frothy creation from her head. "I believe you intended to deceive me all along." She tossed her bonnet onto a little table by the door and set about pulling off her gloves. "I just cannot decide why." Her gloves slapped the tabletop with far more force than was necessary. "So?"

He shook his head. "So....what?" Halting before her, he allowed very little room for her to escape. She'd have to touch him to get around him, or leave by way of the improperly closed door. What an oversight on the oh-so-proper Lady Michaella's part.

"What possible reason could you have had for your deceit?"

What an impossible question to answer! He had more reasons than he could explain even to himself.

"I did not intend to hurt you," he evaded, taking her stiff fingers and closing his around them. "I never wanted that."

"You wanted only to humiliate me?"

Her eyes burned into his, some strange emotion he could not name glimmering deep in those honey gold depths. Did she truly believe him capable of such dishonorable motives?

How could she know? She hardly knew him, did not know anything but what the Derringers had chosen to tell her and he had no idea what they'd divulged. Of course, she'd gotten to know him a little in the time they'd spent together, but how much could one learn of another by flirting?

"Why did you agree to this marriage?"

"Is there to be a marriage?" she countered. Her fingers tightened, briefly, on his before she seemed to recall that he held them. She jerked away, taking a step back. The door stopped her from a complete retreat.

"I will not renege. It is your decision if there will be a marriage or not." He refused to acknowledge the panic that skittered through him at the idea of her rejection. He stepped closer, unable to stop himself even though he knew it might not be wise.

Michaella stared at him, unmoving, no emotion visible in her beautiful features. Clear amber eyes regarded him, whatever he'd seen there earlier far away. She'd scraped her hair ruthlessly tight, twisting it up and away from her face, but a few tendrils had escaped, softening the tension caused by the knot. He found himself reaching out, brushing his bare fingers over her brow, barely feeling the silky strands against his rough skin.

She sighed. He felt the slightest movement, heard the barest whisper of sound, saw the slight tremble of her lips. Her eyes closed, her head leaning just a touch closer to his hand. Rhys felt his body tense at the action, wonder filling him. Did she feel something for him then, something akin to his own stronger than expected feelings for her?

He closed the remaining distance between them. Her eyes snapped open, but she didn't shove him away. He stroked her cheek before sliding his hand behind her neck.

"Why were you so hurt by my deception?" he asked, the words stirring the curls on her brow. "What did you feel that made it so hard to simply laugh and forget about it?"

"You are to be my husband. I would not care to be humiliated every day for the rest of my life."

Her excuse didn't convince him any more than it convinced her. He saw the truth in her eyes. She cared what he thought. She didn't believe it was in his nature to willingly hurt others just as he knew it wasn't in her nature to behave like a shrew. Though she certainly was entitled to, he thought.

"Is that all? I embarrassed you? Your rage was due to embarrassment?" She had no reply, none that she would share with him, but Rhys saw a response quivering on her pretty mouth. Settling his weight on his good leg, he propped his cane against the door behind her and slid his now free hand around her waist. Again, she didn't push him away, allowing the embrace despite the impropriety of their situation.

"Tell me, Michaella, what prompted such righteous indignation?"

"I liked you."

He stared at her. "You liked me?"

Her nod was forced but her body eased against his, distracting him but a moment from the strange revelation he'd just heard.

When no explanation was forthcoming, he prodded, "Care to tell me why that prompted a sennight long cold shoulder?"

"I liked you," she repeated, anger flashing in her eyes. "I liked you, you impossible man! I liked the man I'd come to know, the one who teased me and made light of a physical limitation most men would find humiliating. I liked your strength and your kindness. I liked you!"

Brow furrowing, he interjected, "I still fail to see—"

"I was betrothed to another man but I liked you. What does that say about my loyalty?"

"How can you be loyal to a man you do not know?"

"That does not enter into it! I made a promise and I broke that, in my heart."

"It should enter into it!" His arms tightened around her, unexpected pleasure coursing through him at the mention of her heart. "You cannot give your loyalty to a man you do not know, have never even met. And a man cannot expect that from you, not logically." He searched her face for some sign, some indication that she was really understanding him, hearing what he was not saying. "I did not expect your loyalty, Michaella, not before the vows. I only wanted to know you, wanted you to know me before we officially joined our lives. I did not want a woman who felt constrained to marry me, a woman who would not refuse me only because she felt she'd made an unbreakable promise."

Her eyes glistened with tears but he wasn't sure if she was moved by his words or frightened by his forceful tone. He leaned down, resting his forehead against hers. His eyes drifted shut as he prayed his words would matter, that she'd hear the underlying intensity, the love he was afraid to voice.

A featherlight touch on his lips startled him enough that he lifted his head, eyes shooting wide. "What—"

Her lips silenced his question. Rhys might have wondered at her actions but he was not a man to refuse a gift. He gave up, pulling her close. He'd not experienced such sweetness since his first wife, and that memory was but a pale comparison to the sweetness he received from Lady Michaella's lips. He could happily go on kissing her until the day he died.

Until she dug her fingers into his chest, pulling him closer still, her innocent kiss turning less so. Rhys groaned.

"I assume this means the wedding will be right on

schedule?"

Rhys and Michaella stepped hurriedly apart to face a sardonically amused duke. Michaella would have furthered the distance between them but Rhys slid his arm around her as he reached behind her to retrieve his cane. He pulled her tight to his side and looked Derringer in the eye.

"Were you ever in doubt?" he quipped.

"No, though I did wonder if she would marry you and then shoot you."

"Shoot me?"

Michaella scowled at her brother-in-law. "I would never do something so unladylike," she claimed.

"Can you shoot?" Rhys stared down at her head, waiting for her denial.

She glanced up, eyes twinkling. "Oh yes, of course."

Rhys glared at the duke. "I suppose I have you to thank for that?"

Derringer laughed. "I didn't teach her but I knew she'd learned. Not quite the proper lady you'd thought her, is she?"

Michaella's smile faltered as she gazed at Rhys. He shot her a puzzled frown and said, "I wouldn't know what to do with a proper lady, anyway." He drew her closer. "Now, Duke, would you mind leaving the way you came in"—his eyes shot to the window through which the other man had climbed—"and giving me a moment to properly ask for Michaella's hand?"

"I recommend you lock the door. Bruiser is a busybody."

A grunt from the other side of the drawing room door revealed the butler's presence. Michaella colored up, dipping her head to hide her face in Rhys's coat. Rhys squeezed her tight, smiling despite the annoyance rising to the fore.

"Oh, for the love of— can't you all just go away!"

Derringer bowed, disappearing through the window which he then closed silently behind him. Several moments later, they heard Bruiser's forcible removal from the other side of the door.

Rhys smiled down at his companion. "Now, where were we?"

But Michaella, instead of raising her face to his, stepped away, forcing him to let her go or practically stumble after her.

"I'm not ready for this."

No.

The word shot through Rhys's brain. She was calling off the betrothal.

No.

Forcing calm, he asked, "What? Marriage?"

"Love."

"You love me?"

"I don't know." Her fingers pleated her skirt. She bit her lip. "I loved once and this feels different."

"Different how?" He knew she'd loved the duke's

brother but he'd not expected such a surge of jealousy at her own admission. He was jealous of a dead man.

"With him, I was comfortable. I felt safe, cherished. Content. It nearly destroyed me when he died. I felt all the safety ripped from my life."

Jealousy mixed with confusion and a twinge of disappointment. "And with me you do not feel safe?"

"No," she breathed as if hardly able to keep it to herself. "I do not feel comfortable with you, I feel...tense. I feel...excitement. I—"

He did not allow her to finish. He jerked her back into his arms and took her mouth with far less gentleness than before. Again, she did not pull away but stepped closer, wrapping her arms around him and kissing him back with all that excitement she'd mentioned.

The embrace lasted until Rhys forced himself to break it, forced himself to step back and give her a moment to catch her breath. "That is passion, my love, passion you never felt for your pretty lord." Anger shivered on his words. "He made you feel safe and I make you feel chaos, chaos such as your proper little heart has never had to feel."

He paused, breathing deep, searching for a semblance of calm. He continued, voice lowered. "I don't want you to think I will not protect you with my life but I don't want you to think I will let you deny this"—he gestured at himself and her—"just because you want to do things with me that your proper upbringing has deemed *unsafe*."

Through his diatribe, Michaella had nothing to say. She merely watched him, eyes widening with each word, eyebrows shooting to her hairline as he completed it. When silence settled over them, her lips parted, but instead of speaking she...

Laughed.

Rhys released her, hands dropping to his sides in shock. "My lady?"

Her laughter ceased, fading slowly until nothing remained but a bittersweet smile. "I do not laugh at you, Mr. Wainwright—"

"Rhys."

Smile widening, she conceded, "Rhys." She glanced down at her clasped hands. "As I said, I do not laugh at you... Rhys."

He suspected she smiled again, but she didn't glance up so Rhys couldn't be sure.

"I laugh at myself, at my own...naïveté," she continued, finally raising her eyes. "I loved him." Rhys must have allowed some of his jealousy to show as she spoke. She clasped his hand and tugged him closer. "But," she emphasized, "not in the way I thought."

"Are you sure about that?"

"I am. Now." Her eyes twinkled. "And I very much doubt he loved me anymore than I did him."

"Indeed? How can you be sure of that?" Rhys asked, eyes straying to a rogue lock of hair curling along her cheek. He reached out, tempted to push it behind her ear. Instead, he wound it around his finger, his eyes again settling on her. "I cannot imagine any man who meets you not loving you immensely."

A delightful pink colored her cheeks, but she made no reply. "I may not have loved Gabriel in quite the way you imagine I should have, but I loved what he promised."

Rhys wasn't sure he liked the sound of that. He had money, but nothing compared to what Michaella would have had by marrying into Derringer's family.

But that was absurd! Lady Michaella showed no interest in money, though he assumed she desired a comfortable life. What wife wouldn't?

"And what did his lordship promise?" Rhys forced the words past his lips.

"He said he loved me and wanted to marry me. He promised a peaceful union, children, and a comfortable home. He promised to take me away to the country, where I much prefer to live, and most importantly, he promised that the dangerous life his brother led would not touch us." She shrugged, meeting his gaze with one full of wonder and resignation. "So I loved him too."

"You loved him or the idea that life with him would remain uneventful?"

She glanced away, as if gathering her thoughts in an attempt to answer in a way he'd find satisfactory. With one finger under her chin, he urged her face back to his. "Just tell me, Michaella. Tell me what fascination he held for you. Why were you so determined to love him?"

"Because he treated me as a child. He coddled me. I hadn't felt that way since my father was alive."

Rhys could only stare at her, his hand falling back to his side. His other hand clenched on his cane. Had she really spent years mourning the loss of her true love, not even realizing what she'd felt for the man was nothing more than a familial affection? And she questioned her loyalty?

"My love," he entreated, barely noticing how easily the endearment rolled off his tongue, "do you hear what you are saying? Lord Gabriel St. Clair did not hold your heart. Only your affection."

She shook her head, face stiff with denial, a glimmer of outrage flashing across her face. "I'd have married him."

"I do not doubt it and many Society marriages are based on much less than what you'd have had."

"And I would have been satisfied."

He studied her face, noting the earnestness in her honeyed eyes. She believed what she said and he believed she'd have made Lord Gabriel the perfect wife. She'd have lived and died never knowing what she was capable of feeling.

"And is that what you still desire, a marriage of security and contentment, no excitement?"

"No heartache." Her lip trembled on the words, reminding him just how much she'd suffered the loss of her father and her former love.

"True. You'd have no heartache," he conceded, "and no passion."

"Is passion so important?" she asked.

He thought about that for a moment. He wanted to grab her up, press her body to his, and prove to her just how important passion was. But what would that really prove other than the fact that she desired him as he did her?

He settled for grasping her hand, twining her fingers with his. She glanced up at him, but quickly away, her gaze pinned to their linked hands. Her skirts twitched against his legs, no doubt the product of a tapping foot. He made her nervous? If his feelings were mirrored in his eyes, she'd find him a bit intimidating.

"No, I suppose one can be quite happy without it. But when the possibility for respect, honor, contentment, security, and love is there together with the passion, does it not seem wise to snatch it up, hold onto it for all it's worth?"

Her stunned features shot to his. "Love?"

A smile stretched his lips. "Yes, you delightful girl! Love. Honor. Respect. Contentment. But you can only have these if you accept the passion as well, because I cannot hide how much I desire you, Lady Michaella Harcourt." Her widening grin spurred him on. "Will you do me the very great honor of becoming my wife?" As she started to nod, he added, "Tomorrow?"

Her laughter filled the room. "Yes. Yes, Mr. Wainwright, I will marry you. Tomorrow."

Forgotten

*His heart
belonged
to his past...*

Chapter One

France 1824

Hélène tossed the rag onto the bar, her gaze sliding, as always, down the shining expanse to linger on the man standing at the other end. He laughed with a regular patron, white teeth flashing in his sun-darkened face. He didn't glance her way, but as she watched, his brow furrowed as it always did when he tried to remember something from his past.

Nearly four years ago she'd fished him out of the sea. He remembered nothing of who he was or how he'd come to be there, but ships sank all the time. His accent proclaimed his English roots and his air of superiority hinted at a life amongst the elite. Whether he was nobility or just an upper servant aping his betters was something she couldn't quite decide.

With no hint of his identity and the face of a fallen angel, Hélène could think of no better name than Gabriel. Recalling the look on his face the first time she'd called him that, she knew she'd hit upon something. Recognition, a bit of horror, and a dash of humor darkened his clear blue eyes until they appeared nearly black in his gaunt features. How she'd managed to land on the very name he could lay claim to, or at least one that triggered a memory, was a mystery to her.

She suspected he'd fought in the war that ended nearly a decade past. His absent arm seemed to prove as much, and the way he watched everything, missing so little, was like that of a well-trained soldier, always watching for the sabre aimed at his back.

Pain lurched in Hélène's chest, the ache of a person who cannot bring peace to a loved one. Gabriel's memories were resurfacing but he would not speak of them. And with no desire to really force them from him, she allowed him his secrecy. Her ignorance of his past should have allowed her to be quite happy but she couldn't stop thinking he might have a family somewhere, waiting, grieving. She would certainly grieve his loss were she to find herself suddenly without him.

Retrieving her rag and stowing it under the bar, she

reached for the bucket at her feet and exited through the back door of the tavern.

She failed to note the piercing blue eyes that watched her leave.

"Right looker, that one," a drunk leered, his cloudy eyes following Hélène.

Gabriel chuckled, finally dragging his eyes away from the entrancing woman in order to refill Henri's tankard. "You know better than to say such things about my wife, Henri," Gabriel scolded lightly in flawless French. He attempted a stern face but felt his lips twitch. "She will run you through."

The grizzled old Frenchman chuckled, returning his full attention to his brew. Gabriel grabbed a rag and started polishing the bar, his thoughts far from his task.

Nearly four years had passed since Hélène had found him. He'd been washed ashore, assumed to be the victim of a shipwreck, possessing nothing but the clothes on his back. Hélène took him in, nursed him back to health, and put him to work in her tavern.

Days moved into weeks and weeks into months until a year had passed. Gabriel, with no memories forthcoming, assumed they never would. His relationship with Hélène developed into more than friendship, and with the knowledge of an impending child, he proposed marriage.

She lost the child only days after they married.

Looking back now, Gabriel cringed. Guilt ate at him.

Hélène was a special woman: generous, kind, loyal, strong, and beautiful. In her he'd found a friend with whom he could be himself, this new self he'd had to make out of the fragments of his mind. In her he'd found a connection that kept the darkness at bay.

Until now. He couldn't stop thinking about the fragments of his past that had surfaced, the bits and pieces of memory, places he'd been, and faces he should recognize. Through them all was the face of one person he should know, one person whose face elicited the tenderest of emotions, the strongest of tugs on his heart.

And he couldn't even recall her name.

Henri shoved away from the bar, neglecting to pay his tab again, and doffed his hat, staggering to the door. Gabriel let him go, knowing the man would bed down in one of the outbuildings. During colder months, he slept in the kitchen or the tap.

It was another slow night. The Irish Lion—a ridiculous name for a French tavern—was little more than a hedge tavern, boasting no more than two rooms for let and bringing in only a few loyal patrons. The small building nestled a bit too far from busier thoroughfares to garner any attention from the passing stage.

Resigned to another lean night, Gabriel barred the door and set about cleaning up. He wasn't sure where Hélène had taken herself off to, but he hoped she enjoyed the peace. She worked too long and too hard. His lack of an arm didn't help matters. What a burden he must be!

It hadn't been easy for a one-armed man to be any help to a woman as busy as Hélène, but he'd done his best. And she never complained.

Chapter Two

Hélène settled deeper in the tub, firmly squelching the guilt creeping along the edges of her conscience, and concentrated on the warmth easing her tired muscles. She rarely indulged in a full bath, the burden of carrying the water from the pump outside, heating it, toting it upstairs and then removing the water afterward one bucket at a time, made it almost more work than it was worth. She could have bathed in the kitchen but with Henri still drinking in the tap and no way of knowing how long he'd be doing so, she opted to bathe in her room.

Beside the tub sat a low stool, a single, precious beeswax candle shedding its dim glow over her. She should not burn it, as it was expensive and unlikely to be replaced anytime soon, but the thought of the stinking smoke from a tallow candle put her stomach in knots. Another slow night, financial worries at the fore, with the added burden of another lost child pushed her to the point of needing just a few moments of encompassing warmth.

Her fingers splayed over her empty belly, warm water massaging and caressing her skin. She hadn't bothered to tell Gabriel about this child, so it was her burden to bear alone. Nearly a fortnight had passed, two weeks in which she avoided her husband's embrace, telling him whatever she could to keep him at arm's length. She didn't know how much longer that would last. The bleeding had stopped, finally. She worried that too much longer and he'd suspect the exact thing she sought to keep from him.

Too many times had she seen his face light up, overjoyed at the prospect of becoming a father, only to see that joy fade with each loss. It made her wonder about his past. Was he a father already, with a grieving wife and children awaiting his return? What a sad thought.

Her womb was not made for babies, a feminine failing her late husband had used to berate her. She'd comforted herself at the time with the thought that her womb didn't want his babies. Now, she had to acknowledge the truth. She could not have children, not even those of a fallen angel.

Disgusted, she fisted her hands, the sudden movement sending a wave of water over the side. She'd have to clean that up later but at the moment, she couldn't care. Anger mixed with despair. A tavern was no place to rear children anyway, she told herself. She must be content with the hand fate had dealt her, namely a tavern that managed to keep itself afloat and a handsome husband to help her run it.

A husband who would have to close up on his own if she didn't move herself to action soon. With a hearty sigh, Hélène rose from the tub, allowing the water to sluice down her body. She reached for a linen towel, wrapping it snuggly around her and stepping to the bare wooden floor. A small fire burned in the grate, a meager offering only there to warm the slight chill in the air.

She dried herself as quickly as she could, shivering as she did so. A soft nightrail battled the chill and she sat on the bed to brush out her deep red hair. The exercise soothed her frayed nerves, to the point that soon she could barely hold the brush. Sighing, weary beyond words, she set it aside, lying down. She was asleep before she remembered she'd neglected to take care of the tub.

Gabriel entered their bedchamber, the small room swathed in the dim glow of the one candle burning on a stool beside the wash tub. He smiled. She'd taken a moment to indulge in a bath, something she rarely found time to do.

His gaze swept the room, settling on his wife in their bed. Her face relaxed in sleep, he marveled at her beauty.

Red curls spilled over the white linens, partially obscuring the classic beauty of her face. Her nightrail hid most of her body, a body he knew all too well, all lush curves and softness. He missed her willing touch, her passionate embrace. And he wondered at her distance.

The bath would need to be emptied, he mused. Never one to eschew an opportunity for bathing—something he'd learned in the war—Gabriel shed his clothes as quickly as was possible with only one hand and no obliging wife. He sank down into the lukewarm water. His thoughts swirled, hazy memories advancing and retreating like so many wraiths. He'd remembered the war, losing his arm, just as he'd remembered far more of his past. Bits and pieces fell into place, some nothing more than trifling things, others so hazy that he had nothing more than a faint recollection of people or places.

Another face stuck in his head, a mirror image of his own, the same overlong black hair tied back at the nape and harsh features, but with obsidian eyes instead of his own clear blue. The man must be a relation. Who else could resemble him so closely?

The hour grew late, the water grew cold, and Gabriel shook his head to clear his murky thoughts. He'd have to go about emptying the bath. A deep sigh, one part relief and one part resignation, swelled his lungs. He could leave it for morning. Hélène would clean it up, saying naught to him. She'd never complain.

He glanced over at her sleeping form. She deserved so much better than the life she led.

Determined to make at least this part easier, Gabriel rose, pulled his breeches on, and went about the time-consuming task of emptying the bath. It wasn't the easiest task for his wife with her two hands. For him, one arm absent to the shoulder, it was messy indeed.

After the third bucket of water he dipped sloshed over the already damp floor boards, he swore, his tone loud enough to disturb the woman in the bed.

"Gabriel, whatever are you doing?" she asked. Her sleep clouded voice sent a shaft of desire snaking through him. His reaction to her now was the same as it had been when she'd fished him from the water all those years ago. Desire, raw, needy, pulsating, filling his veins with molten heat, clamoring for release.

He forced the desire back to a controllable degree, annoyed he'd disturbed her much-needed slumber. "My apologies, dear heart," he soothed, cursing himself in four languages and only mildly surprised that he could.

Hélène sat up, her thick burnished curls falling over one shoulder. "I can do that," she remonstrated, sliding off the bed to join him by the nearly empty tub. A smile wreathed her lovely features, the glimmerings of which Gabriel could just see in the flickering candlelight. "You only succeed in making more of a mess, *chéri*," she teased, taking the bucket from his hand.

As she bent down to fill the bucket herself, her thin nightrail pulled taut across her back, curving over her bottom. Gabriel stared, unable to suppress his desire any longer. It had been too long, he thought, since he'd held her, made love to her as if the world might end on the morrow. He touched her spine, startling her enough that she swung about, nearly hitting him with the bucket she still clutched. Water splashed all around them, her ready smile breaking forth.

"Shame on you, impossible man!" she scolded, the teasing note in her voice deepened with more than just sleep.

Arm sliding around her waist, he pulled her close. He fitted her curves against him with the ease of familiarity. "Forget the wash tub, love." Hélène tipped her head up at his words, her hair falling back to expose her neck. He pressed his lips to the delicate skin just under her ear, breathing in the scent of soap and lavender, warmth and something uniquely Hélène. He sighed against her skin. "I have a better idea."

Hélène melted. Gabriel felt her capitulation in every muscle in her body. Ease and tension hummed along her flesh, her fingers clutching his shoulder. He kissed his way to her lips, tasting her, teasing her, reveling in the connection, plundering her lips with single-minded absorption.

The bucket in her hand thumped to the floor, spilling the

rest of its contents across the worn wood.

Chapter Three

England beckoned.

Gabriel sat up in bed, breathing hard. He stared into nothing, the darkness complete. Sensation in his arm ranged from minor tingles to stabbing pains. Reaching over he discovered it wasn't there, thus couldn't possibly feel what it was feeling.

Wiping his hand over his face, the limb trembled. He thought he'd be sick. Hélène slept the sleep of the innocent beside him. Her mind did not roil with half-memories of war and lost family. She didn't need to fear her own thoughts, fear the hazy recollections teasing the edges of her consciousness.

Some nights he'd wake, like now, an overwhelming desire to see England singing through his veins. He knew France could not claim his heritage, even if his French was flawless. Hélène knew his roots screamed of the British

Isles; she accepted him despite such a huge flaw in his character.

He smiled at the memory of their wedding night, when she'd declared as much to him.

But now, the urge to return overwhelmed him. There were things there, people there, who knew him, would know who he was and what happened to him.

He would know the truth. Rising as carefully as possible to avoid disturbing his wife, he pulled on his breeches and moved across the small chamber. He stepped around the neglected wash basin, his feet taking him to the one window in the room. Light seeped through the crack in the shutters. He pushed them wide. Dawn bled pink across the horizon, spilling its light into the room.

The English Channel glimmered blue and green in the dawn light. Gabriel saw but didn't see. What he saw, deep in his mind's eye, was the same water but from a different shore.

"Dover."

He spun about, meeting the far too shrewd gaze of his better half. She stood before him, vibrant hair spilling about her pale shoulders as her hands clutched the sheet wrapped around her naked body. Her eyes were trained on him rather than the stunning view that greeted them nearly every morning. In those deep blue orbs lay a plethora of questions, an ocean of uncertainty.

No longer able to meet her concerned gaze, Gabriel

returned to the window. A boat made its leisurely way through the water, nothing more than a speck in the blue and green. A visitor from England, no doubt.

"Dover is not so far."

The words whispered over him, the tone in which they were uttered saying far more than the words themselves. He faced her again, hand hanging limply at his side.

"It is not, but everything else is," he responded, saying the only thing he could. "Dover is but a sea away. Everything else exists much, much further."

She approached on silent feet, her bare toes peeking out with each step she took. It only took three for her to reach his side. "Gabriel," she said, pressing her slender hand against his bare chest, "you do not belong here. You are not French and you are not the class of a tavern owner. You belong in England, with English people, and English ways. You belong with the English nobility."

"What have I said or done to make you think I am nobility?" he demanded, knowing just how much she despised the entitled upper echelons of French Society. Her grandfather had helped many French noblemen and women to their deaths, personally introducing them to Madame Guillotine. She was raised in the belief that the French nobility cared for no one but themselves. How much more could she despise the unknown English?

Her shrug sent a lock of hair sliding down over her arm. Gabriel watched its progress, his fingers itching to follow in its wake. "Perhaps your snobbish English ways," she teased. A smile fluttered over her full lips, but never fully formed.

He grinned, snaking his arm around her and pulling her close. "I think you enjoy my snobbish English ways."

She kissed him, a half-hearted salute that was over before it really began. "I enjoy you, *chéri*, very much. But you are not happy. I need you to be happy."

"What are you suggesting?" He pulled her in for another kiss, prolonging the embrace until her knees weakened and she sagged against him. He smiled against her lips, but her next words, whispered into his kiss, spilled icy water over his desire.

"I am selling the tavern, Gabriel."

He released her. She scrambled to maintain hold of her sheet and stay upright, barely managing. Her sheet loosened, slipped lower, revealing the tops of her breasts.

He ignored all that. "Selling the tavern? Why?"

"You must travel to England and for that you need money."

"You can't do that! If I want to go to England, I will find a way. I will not take the only thing you own." His indignation knew no bounds. How dare she consider giving him everything just so he could go on some wild chase, seeking out his past in some fanciful desire to know who and what he was!

The phantom woman rose to taunt him, her soft brown

curls framing her round, sweetly smiling features. Why was her face so clear but her name so elusive? And why did guilt shroud the memory?

"It is my tavern and if I wish to sell it, I shall."

Rubbing at the furrows in his brow, he fought for an answer. Hélène possessed a stubborn streak unlike anything Gabriel had ever known. If she was determined to get him to England, to England he would go.

He spun back to stare over the water. He knew he had to go but he did not have to take everything she had. What if the worst happened and he found the woman in his dreams was in fact his wife? He could not, in good conscience, abandon her to return to his French wife, no more than he could abandon his French wife with no means of supporting herself. He should never have married her with no knowledge of his past. He never should have touched her.

He glanced over his shoulder to find her watching him steadily. "Promise me that you will wait. Let us see what information England provides before taking such a step."

Her eyes narrowed, just the slightest, not truly alarming but enough to tell him she saw through his excuse. Nevertheless, she nodded. "I will wait."

His response was nothing more than a nod as he turned back to the window. She stepped up beside him, sidling her way between him and the window, leaning back into his chest and forcing him to wrap his arm around her. He had no objection, inhaling her warm, lavender scent. If it wasn't for the woman in his dreams he was quite sure he could love Hélène. Why hadn't he remembered her sooner, long before he'd asked the entrancing Frenchwoman to marry him?

Chapter Four

The tavern opened, as usual, the following day. Hélène stood behind the bar, wiping glasses and surreptitiously watching Gabriel as he wiped down the few tables in the tap. He seemed brighter somehow, lighter, as if a weight was lifted from his conscience. Or perhaps she was wishful of such a circumstance. It was because of her that he worried at all. If not for her, he'd be on the next boat to England, determined to fill in the missing bits of his memory.

She'd lied to him the night before, telling him she'd wait to sell the tavern. It was already sold. The new owner would take possession by the end of the week.

Their lives were about to change and she was ready for it. There was no use railing against change, fate, destiny, or whatever one chose to call it. It happened. Hélène knew that better than most. She would move with change instead of against it. It was why she encouraged the man she loved to search out the family *he* loved. It was the correct thing to do.

Even if it killed her.

He glanced up, as if he could feel her watching him, and the lightness she sensed before disappeared. His brow furrowed, muscles tightening along his shoulders for just a moment. The look passed and he offered her a lopsided grin. He returned to his work and she returned to hers.

A moment later, he left the tap and went to the kitchen. Hélène didn't ask why. She left the bar and made sure the tap was as neat and clean as possible before they opened the doors for the two or three patrons who would find their way in that day.

It wasn't long before the smells of frying eggs, sizzling bacon, and fragrant coffee filled the small tavern. Hélène smiled, remembering how difficult it had been to teach a one-armed man to make his own breakfast. She'd been willing to cook for him, but he'd insisted. His feelings of worthlessness had always been apparent, so she humored him whenever possible. He'd learned quickly and efficiently.

He'd also learned patience. An impatient man learning to cook with one hand was likely to get burned.

Taking one last swipe at a resistant spot on the table before her, she turned, her feet taking her to the kitchen. On the table lay a feast of eggs, toast, and bacon, steaming cups of coffee adding to the aromatic ambiance. Gabriel crouched beside the fire, turning just enough to smile at her as she tossed her rag down beside her plate.

"Breakfast, *chéri*? You will make me fat." And though she smiled at him, she wished deep down that she would grow fat, fat with his child. That would never be, however, and she must accept that.

His chuckle sent a warm tingle through her veins. "You, Hélène? You will never grow fat, love. You never stop moving long enough for fat to gather." He joined her, taking her hand in his and lacing their fingers together. "I would not object, if you did. I'd love to see you fat and happy, one child at your breast while another plays at your feet." He drew her close, and Hélène went willingly, though her heart hurt for the dream he had. It was not to be their dream.

It took a supreme effort of will, but Hélène managed to not put a protective hand over her empty womb.

It mattered not. Despite spending the night in her arms, making love as if they'd only just married, Gabriel had only one thing on his mind and it wasn't breakfast. He pushed her back against the edge of the table, his lips on her neck, his hand curving around her waist to pull her against the muscled wall of his chest. Her heart kicked up a beat, desire clouding all else from her mind.

Just as Gabriel's hand slid down over her hip, she stiffened, every muscle tensing. Somewhere in her mind, a warning sounded, a mild acknowledgment that there was something else there, some sound that didn't fit with the low crackle of the kitchen fire or the labored breathing of her companion. But Gabriel didn't hear and continued his assault on her senses, rendering her once again oblivious to their surroundings.

Thunk.

The sound sent them stumbling apart. Hélène's hands grasped for the table edge, her shaking legs needing the support. She watched Gabriel's face drain of color, his ear cocked toward the tap.

"Thieves," he breathed.

Hélène felt her heart drop. Thieves? In her tavern? But it wasn't her tavern anymore and if thieves destroyed the place, the new owner would renege on the deal. She couldn't let that happen!

On that thought, she catapulted from the table, across the kitchen and through the door. The sight that met her eyes sent desolation straight through her.

Two men, one short and muscular like a pugilist, the other tall and boasting the looks of a blond god, stood in the middle of the tavern, eyeing the large chandelier hanging from the beams above. The tall one gestured up, saying over his shoulder, "If it's anywhere, it's up there. She talked about the bloody thing more than such a hideous piece warrants."

Hélène couldn't think what they hoped to find up there,

but she knew she couldn't let them destroy it. It was nothing of real value, but it was something her husband put up, all those years ago, back when she thought love was the reason for their marriage. Perhaps it was. It mattered little now.

She didn't think. Snatching the short pistol she kept primed under the bar, she strode forward.

"You will leave, at once." Her French held a note of the gutter, a tone she could use if she wanted, but often did not, preferring to sound a bit more refined.

The men turned, regarding her with surprise. "The tavern was to be empty," the tall man informed her. He glanced at his companion.

Hélène felt Gabriel step up behind her. But he didn't stop there. He strode purposefully into the tap, stopping a few feet from the tall man. "We are not yet open for the day. Please leave."

The man snorted. "I am not afraid of you, Heartless. What do I care if you find my presence here offensive? You are scum here and in England."

Gabriel did not back down, though his brow furrowed at the name the man called him. Hélène's heart sunk to her toes as she saw the telltale signs of stubborn resolve in her husband's stance.

Hélène studied the intruders, something in the man's stance vaguely familiar. He had the manner of a lord and his accent declared him to be British, though she detected a hint of French, as if he attempted to hide his true heritage. In her experience, a nob intent on hiding his true self had nefarious purposes in mind. The way he watched them gave her the impression that he was not used to being denied. She didn't trust him and it wasn't only because he invaded her domain.

Gabriel's voice lowered, just a touch, a certain silky quality entering his tone that she'd never have considered frightening before now. "You do not know me and you are not welcome here. Kindly leave."

The tall man snorted and gestured one long-fingered, white hand at his large companion. "Hugo, show his grace we mean business."

Hugo stepped forward, but Gabriel was full of surprises. He didn't move, waiting for the other man to get within a foot of him. Then he attacked.

In a flurry of movement, the stocky henchman was subdued. Hélène stood frozen, the pistol a lead weight in her hand as she observed her husband atop the unconscious brute. The tall man stared as well, his own shock writ plain across his white face. He glanced from Gabriel to the brute and then at Hélène.

"This is unacceptable."

In his tone, Hélène heard something sinister. Her gaze snapped to him, sliding over his form to determine the threat. Gabriel rose from his perch, advancing on the other man.

"Will you leave now?" he asked with perfect calm.

The man shook his head and smiled. "I am afraid not." His hand snapped up. A deafening blast rent the air around them. Hélène's hand shuddered for a moment, then fell to her side. She dropped to her knees, the gun she held clattering to the floor.

Gabriel sped to her side. "Hélène?"

She moved her head in the direction of his voice. "Is he dead?"

"Yes. How did you—?"

"I'm a crack shot, I think you English call it." Her smile wavered. "I've never shot a man before." The contents of her stomach threatened to emerge, but Hélène fought it.

It was necessary.

It was sickening.

He'd have killed Gabriel.

She killed him.

Gabriel left her side for a moment, searching the body of the thin man. He pulled something out of the man's pocket. Hélène watched him, her eyes on him while her concentration remained on the battle of wills she fought with her stomach.

"This is bad," Gabriel muttered, meeting her gaze. He held up a calling card. "Darling, meet the Marquis de Leroux. You've killed a French nobleman."

She lost the battle.

Chapter Five

They escaped into the night. With only a few essential items, they fled, knowing Hélène could not stand trial for the death of a nobleman. Gabriel would not see her hang for protecting him.

He also could not forget the man's belief that Gabriel was someone called Heartless. Who could such a person be? Someone he knew, perhaps?

And there was something else he found, another mystery. As Hélène readied their clothing, he'd headed into the kitchen to gather some food. But something drew him to the tap, his gaze locking on the chandelier. Those men were convinced something was hidden up there. But what could it be? Nothing large could possibly be hidden there. Something small, perhaps? Maybe a document of some sort?

The table before him was large, heavy, certainly sturdy enough to hold his weight. He gave it a shove, sliding it a few feet until it was centered under the chandelier. He clambered atop the thing, nearly losing his balance. Grasping the chandelier, he felt in all the little crevices, his fingers searching for anything that was out of place.

His search was not easy. The inability to hold the swinging chandelier with one hand while searching with the other was frustrating. To add insult to injury, he found nothing.

Now they fled on foot, intent on finding someone to take them across the channel to find sanctuary with the English. Gabriel didn't know how Hélène would survive in a country amongst people she seemed to despise, but they had no choice.

A cold night wind blew in, sending chills over them both.

Hélène stood beside Gabriel, waiting for the boat that would take them to England, her heart hammering in her chest. In her hand she clutched their one bag, and in her pocket was secreted a diamond brooch.

The man she shot weighed heavily on her mind and not just because she'd killed him. She knew what he'd been looking for. She couldn't begin to understand why he thought it was in the chandelier, no matter what he thought his wife said about it.

The captain was late. Gabriel kept glancing over his

shoulder, as if expecting the authorities to swoop down on them at any moment.

Hélène took the opportunity to reveal the brooch to her husband, pressing it into his hand. "I think they wanted this."

Gabriel glanced down at the thing, barely able to see it in the dim moonlight. "A brooch? Why were they after this?"

"It's covered in diamonds. Blue ones."

His jaw dropped. "Blue diamonds? How did you come by it?"

"It was—"

The captain appeared in that moment, sending them into a flurry of activity. Gabriel stuffed the brooch into the bag on her arm, saying nothing more about it. Hélène saw no need to remind him.

One night on board the small boat taking them to Dover resulted in nightmare after nightmare. Pistols, churning water, and the horror of knowing one was about to die coalesced to form one giant miasma of terror, culminating in the faces of the men who watched it all happen.

He sat up straight. "Brother?" He blinked slowly and shook his head. "Cousin?"

Hélène's hand slid over his thigh, the comforting action barely registering in his mind. "Brother, *chéri*? Have you remembered a brother?"

"Or a cousin? Both, perhaps." His eyes settled on the lone porthole in the tiny cabin. "I'm not sure. But I think...I remember dying."

Hélène, sleep-fogged and drowsy, came fully awake. "You remember the shipwreck?"

He shook his head. "Murder. My brother...I think...tried to kill me. Perhaps it was my cousin. Two men, one dark, one light, and I don't know which is my brother and which is my cousin. I don't even remember their names. I only remember their faces, that I knew them, but not as well as I should have."

She heard the frustration coating each word, felt the tension all along the hard muscles of his thigh. His hand fisted in his lap. Sliding her hand over, she grasped his hand, forcing his fingers apart. The boat rocked gently, such a soothing motion, but Gabriel's tension began to feed into her, setting up a fluttering in her stomach that threatened to spill forth.

"I would take it all from you, if I could," she whispered. He turned to look at her, the dull, early morning light spilling through the porthole not enough to show her the expression on his face. "I would take the memories so you could live in peace."

He jerked away from her. She knew her harsh words would not be well-received but the violence of his reaction startled her.

"You would take my memories instead of restoring them?" he demanded. He flung himself from the bunk, pulling on his outer clothing as quickly as he could with only one hand.

She sat up. "I would! You are miserable with the pieces you have remembered. What would the memories do for you?"

"Tell me who I am! Why someone wanted me to die!" He swept his hand out, frustration evident on the tense movement. "I would have answers! I would not have to wonder, still, if there is anyone out there who waits for me, grieving, wondering if Derringer made a bloody mistake when he returned without me!"

Hélène's heart stuttered. "Derringer? The black duke?" Could it be so? Was her husband related to the worst nobleman to ever call England home? "Lord Heartless?" She studied Gabriel. She couldn't say if there was a resemblance, having never make the duke's acquaintance, but if it was true...

The expression on Gabriel's face told her he had as little knowledge of his relationship to the duke as she did. He said nothing, his thoughts turned inward, and she could do nothing but watch as he tried to remember something as elusive as a wisp.

One wasn't always welcomed when arriving in Dover

and this was no different. Gabriel and Hélène stepped off the boat with their few belongings, alone except for the strangers milling about them.

"Come, my dear," Gabriel murmured, firmly grasping their bag and offering his elbow to his wife. "We must go to London, I think."

"London?"

He glanced down at her. "Have you never wanted to see the City?"

Hélène shook her head. "I haven't the opportunity to think of such things. The tavern took all my attention, *chéri*."

He cringed at the reminder. He thought little of things such as visiting another country and now he wondered why. It was clear his roots lay in the well-to-do, the ones who traveled the globe with no thought for the cost of such travel. He'd had more than one conversation with his wife that revealed as much.

Silence reigned as they made their way to an inn nearby. Gabriel turned toward the larger establishment with little thought, while his wife moved toward a lesser establishment that clearly catered to a lower class of patrons. Without a word, Gabriel sighed and settled their sack of belongings more comfortably on his shoulder. Hélène squeezed his arm, attuned to his every mood.

"We will find your people, *chéri*," she soothed, "and you can return to your fancy inns and carriages. For now, we must make do with less."

Her touch warmed him even as her words sent a chill through his veins. He needed to remember that no matter where he came from, his new circumstances were the reality.

Pulling his wife closer to his side, they entered the Boar's Head.

Chapter Six

It was several days of hard travel later that they entered London. Very little of the City brought up memories. Gabriel could only conclude he'd spent little time there. And after viewing the City from the roof of the mail coach —in the drenching rain—Gabriel was quite sure he'd happily live the rest of his days without ever seeing it again. Hélène shivered next to him, snuggling closer under his arm in an effort to withstand the chill.

The mail coach stopped at a small building that one might generously call an inn. Gabriel helped Hélène inside, cringing at the smell of boiled cabbage and stale smoke.

He would have protested staying in such a place but Hélène sailed forward, taking over where she was much more qualified than he was, charming the taciturn landlord into allowing them to bed down in the tap, though it went against the man's normal practice. Returning to Gabriel's side, she sidled up to him, a teasing light entering her eyes as she whispered, "Men desire praise, my love, that is all. And they will eat out of your hand."

Gabriel's eyes slid over his wife's generous curves, settling on the rich bounty displayed above the top of her bodice. "Methinks an ample bosom helps," he quipped, meeting her eyes and smiling.

Hélène chuckled and squeezed his arm, pulling him gently with her as she moved across the small room. "Our generous host shall bring bread and cheese in but a moment's time, then we shall sleep. You shall keep me safe tonight, *chéri*, and tomorrow we shall continue our journey."

Her no-nonsense attitude went far in soothing Gabriel's pent-up nerves. Each day had its own worries and Hélène knew how to keep the morrow's worries firmly in the morrow. He envied her ability, his thoughts so consumed in his lack of memories that he often forgot where he was or what he was doing.

Now that his memories were returning, he wondered if that constant worry would pass, or worsen. Only time would tell.

They walked, their money all but gone. Neither noticed the long trek, nor mentioned the hot sun beating down on them. It was nothing new to Hélène and something Gabriel had become accustomed to.

They approached Westminster Abbey, the bells ringing out gaily, heralding the joining of two souls in matrimony. A passing wish for the goodwill of whichever souls happened to be uniting was the only thought Gabriel gave the situation. But Hélène paused, drawing him to a stop amongst the others gathered there. People milled about, some there out of curiosity, others hopeful beggars.

Hélène did not react the way most women did. Instead of sighing over the idea of marriage, she smirked up at him. "Is it a young bride, do you think, her husband an aging *roue* with blunt to spare?"

"I haven't the least idea," Gabriel admitted, "nor do I care."

Hélène laughed. "Come, *chéri*! Have you not the slightest interest in who might be in there, pledging themselves to each other before God and man?"

He didn't but he could see Hélène was curious. "If you wish to wait and see who it is, I have no objection." Her smile warmed him. "I do not see what the interest is, however, when it is unlikely you know them."

"Oh, *chéri*, I don't need to know them. I merely need to see them. I find the nobility of great interest, you see."

Gabriel's heart sank. "What do you hope to gain?" he asked, turning them so he could not see the church doors. "My past may be nothing more than that of an upper servant, of no account and long since forgotten by his master."

Hélène stepped closer, tipping her head up to better meet his eyes. "I know who you are," she whispered. "The pieces are all there, and you have but to place them in the correct order. I have already done so. You will too."

Before he could form a response, the church doors burst open, people spilling out into the street. Gabriel swiveled his head, barely seeing anything amidst the throng.

And then he saw *her.*

All the air left his lungs. He struggled to draw a breath. Brown curls framing a round, radiant face. Brown eyes of a lighter hue, all manners and grace, a pure lady, through and through. The girl from his dreams, the girl he'd left behind. She strode from the church on the arm of a man, her ready smile directed at her new husband.

He couldn't believe what he was witnessing. Lady Michaella Harcourt. Married.

Lost to him forever.

The magnitude of what just happened slamming him in the chest, Gabriel turned away. His feet took him across the square, into a small stand of trees. There he stopped, bracing his hand on his knee, sucking in great lungfuls of air, fighting the blackness threatening to send him into oblivion.

He knew her. He loved her. Once. She was all that was perfect in a young lady. Modest, polite, graceful, meek.

The perfect lady, the perfect wife.

She'd promised to marry him. But before they could tell their families, he'd been kidnapped along with Derringer, then shot by the man he'd believed to be his brother and thrown overboard. He'd washed ashore in France, mostly dead, remembering nothing.

How he wished he still remembered nothing!

"*Chéri?*"

Hélène's soft tones washed over him. The panic receded, leaving a dull resignation in its wake. He stood, leaning into the tree at his back.

"You remember?"

He could do nothing more than nod. Unmanly tears stung his eyes but he wasn't sure why. Was it the loss of Michaella? Or the memory of his brother's betrayal?

Hélène's fingers squeezed his. "Come, *chéri*. It is time for us to go."

Gabriel could think of no objection. He fell into step beside her.

Chapter Seven

Hélène knew what she had to do. The final piece had fallen into place, confirming what she'd but suspected. Gabriel's reaction to his love's marriage was enough to solidify her resolve. Digging through her reticule, she found just enough money to hire a hackney to take them to the Duke of Derringer's London residence. Gabriel would find all his answers there.

Her unresisting husband remained silent, his thoughts turned deeply inward. She wished she could ease his pain, bring him some relief from the torment.

The conveyance stopped before a tall, red bricked townhouse, nothing about it declaring it different from the ones on either side of it. Hélène knew it was the correct one, however. Flirting was an effective means of securing information and if there was one thing Hélène knew, it was how to flirt.

A less generous soul might call it manipulation.

She paid the hackney driver and took their bag, shepherding her husband up the wide steps to the front door. It might be easier to go round back and gain entrance by way of the servants, but Hélène didn't care. She beat a rapid tattoo on the heavy door and waited.

The butler—a short, squat, ugly man with a face like a bulldog—opened the door. He glanced at Hélène, looked her over, then said, "The master don't keep comp'ny wit the likes o' you."

He'd have shut the door but Gabriel regained his powers of speech. "Give over, Bruiser, you ugly cur! Take us to Hart and apologize to my wife."

Bruiser's gaze shot to Gabriel's face. He stuttered out some incoherent reply, then turned and fled up the stairs.

They watched him go. Hélène shrugged and hefted her bag up. "He did not bar the door. Perhaps we are welcome."

Gabriel grunted. "The bloody makebait. He's the worst butler known to man. If he wasn't so good at saving Hart's miserable neck, he'd not be kept around, I assure you."

Hélène said nothing, merely led the way inside.

As they glanced around the foyer, Bruiser returned, still visibly flustered but calmer than before. Bowing, he addressed Hélène first, "Beggin' pardon, madam." Then he turned to Gabriel and muttered, "Duke's gone to the weddin'. Blue room's yers, if yer stayin'." He bowed again, and shuffled off in the direction of the kitchens.

Gabriel stared up toward part of the house Bruiser indicated. He sighed. "I'm not sure I quite remember where the blue room is," he admitted.

Hélène shrugged again. "Then we poke our noses into each room until we find it."

"It's not blue," Gabriel supplied helpfully, his eyes dancing over her upturned features with a hint of merriment. "It's yellow."

"I despise yellow."

"I know."

Hélène smiled and nodded. "Very well then. Let us proceed."

They found the room and settled in. Bruiser knocked twenty minutes later, offering a tea tray. Hélène's stomach rumbled at the sight of cakes, biscuits, and thick slices of ham on buttered bread. Offering Bruiser the biggest smile of thanks, she then shut the door in his face.

"That was rude," Gabriel remarked.

"No. Was it?" Hélène's shrug said nothing and everything at the same time. "He was rude to me." Gazing back at the door, she wondered aloud, "Do you think he'd fetch me a bath?"

Gabriel threw open the door as Hélène set the tray on the table by the window. "Bruiser!" he bellowed, the sound echoing through the house. Gabriel glanced over his shoulder at Hélène, watching her poke through the food on the tray.

The man appeared with eerie promptness, his deep voice startling Gabriel. "Milord?"

The mode of address startled Gabriel more than Bruiser's sudden appearance. He'd never had the chance to get used to being a lord. He was Derringer's younger brother, his twin, in fact, but he'd been raised as a cousin to prevent the possibility of a fight over the dukedom. In an odd twist of irony, Martin, the man Gabriel had always considered his brother, had coveted the title for himself and taken steps to make it happen.

Gabriel shook these memories away, focusing on the man before him. "My wife desires a bath."

Bruiser frowned, grunted, and departed.

"I think he is fetching it," Gabriel said, not entirely sure of the truth of his claim. He glanced at Hélène to find her watching him, a sad little frown drawing her brows into a V above her troubled blue eyes.

He crossed the room and drew her to him, his arm wrapped around her waist to pull her close. Dropping a kiss on her forehead, he soothed, "It will all work out, love. I promise."

Hélène forced a smile and pushed away from him. With a deftness that spoke of years serving others, she urged him to sit and placed a brandy and a plate of food on the table before him. "The man has brains, even if he hasn't looks," she acknowledged, dipping her head in the direction of the brandy.

"And Derringer has taste," Gabriel mused, savoring the expensive French beverage he held. The alcohol curled around his stomach, sending rivulets of heat throughout his limbs.

His mind tripped over the day's events, Michaella's wedding the foremost thought in his mind. He could not forget the joy on her face, the radiance that she'd once reserved only for him. She bestowed that on another man now, a man Gabriel hadn't bothered to notice at the time. Who was this man she married, this man she used to forget about him? Jealousy and desolation warred in his mind, woven with shame. He quaffed his brandy and poured another, praying for oblivion.

A weary lassitude overcame him, sleep fighting for dominance.

He must have dozed. He woke to the sound of Hélène's soothing voice.

"Come, *chéri*," Hélène murmured. "The bath is arrived and I am finished. Refresh yourself."

Gabriel obediently rose, the drowsiness he felt dissipating as his wife helped him undress, each movement a slow, sensuous act that sent his senses spiraling. He shook the feeling away, climbing into the lukewarm water.

He might have dozed again but for Hélène's attentive ministrations to his person. Every time he felt his eyes drift shut, her hands slid over him, awakening more than just his consciousness. She teased and tormented, dragging a groan from him that was edged with a feral growl.

He could finally take no more, surging from the water and stepping from the tub in a swift movement that nearly knocked her on her backside. She smiled, the minx knowing exactly what she was about. He didn't smile back. He grasped her arm none too gently and slammed her into his chest, kissing her in a way that left little doubt as to his intentions.

Chapter Eight

"She does not deserve you, *chéri*."

Hélène's words whispered over his chest as he held her in the aftermath of their frenzied lovemaking. She knew, then, that his attentions to her had less to do with her and more to do with guilt over another woman. Guilt ate at him and he had no response.

She lifted her head, thick red curls falling over her eyes. Pushing them impatiently away, she added, "Had she loved you, *chéri*, she'd have found you. Not sat back and mourned a loss that might not have been."

"My own brother thought I was dead, Hélène," he reminded her. "He searched for me once and found me. When he saw me die before his very eyes..." His sigh fluttered the hair on her brow. "They cannot be blamed for believing me dead. Michaella cannot be blamed for moving on with her life, marrying another man. One wonders why she waited so long."

She snorted. "I'd never have believed you dead. I'd have searched for you 'til the day I died."

There was so much more in her tone than her words revealed but she continued before he could say a word about it.

"Can you let her go now? She is married. She is happy."

The guilt still ate at him but she was right. Michaella was married, happy. He'd seen the way she smiled at the man she now called husband. But...

"What if she's not? Happy, I mean?"

Hélène's snort assaulted his ears. "Did you see her husband? Very fair of face and looking at her as if he would eat her alive. They are happy, *chéri*, and tonight he is showing her exactly how much he desires her." She rubbed her hand over his stubbled cheek. "Much the way you should be showing me. Only me." Her hand slid down over his chest. He sucked in a breath as her clever fingers played him like a harp, taunting and teasing until he no longer cared who Michaella was.

Gabriel awoke, memories of the night just past awakening more than just his mind. He reached over to pull Hélène to him, intent on making love to her again, while his mind remained focused entirely on her and not some pretty dream of a perfectly calm, passionless life with the perfect lady he once knew.

His hand came up empty.

His gaze slid over the pillow beside him, the lack of indentation indicating his companion had not been there for some time. Where the devil would she go? Even now, the sun was barely up, gray light only beginning to filter through the part in the heavy gold curtains.

She was probably searching for food. Hélène had an appetite she'd not had before. Instinct told him she was increasing, his rather extensive knowledge of her person merely confirming that instinct.

Ah well. She could search the townhouse if she wanted. Derringer wouldn't mind, he was sure.

He pushed up onto his elbow. Black hair fell over his eyes and he moved to brush it back. A groan ripped from his throat at the action. The times he forgot his crippled state were fewer and fewer but there were still occasions when he attempted something only possible with two hands.

"Bloody hell," he muttered, sitting up.

"Problems, brother?"

Gabriel's eyes shot to the darkened corner of the room. A shadow sat in a chair, unmoving.

"Hart?"

"Have you another brother?" was the amused reply.

Gabriel grunted. "I suppose not."

The shadow rose, moving to the single window and drawing the drapes. He turned, favoring Gabriel with an assessing look. "You appear in good health," he remarked.

Gabriel ignored this. "Where is my wife?"

Derringer's brows rose. "Bruiser was not mistaken. The doxy is your wife."

The sudden urge to lay Derringer out, pummel him to within an inch of his life, surged up in Gabriel's breast. He suspected it wasn't all on Hélène's behalf. "She is not a doxy. She's a French tavernkeeper."

Derringer stared at him silently for a long moment, then nodded. "Very well. She is not a doxy. She is a respectable woman." He paused. "And your wife."

Gabriel nodded. "Good. May I rise? Or is there more you need to know?"

"Just one more thing," Derringer drawled, stepping up next to the bed.

Gabriel was finally given the opportunity to really look at the duke. He appeared unchanged, every article of clothing as black as the long hair brushing his shoulders. But a long, thin scar graced the left side of his face. That was new.

"Have you always been so ugly, Gabe?"

Gabriel muttered an obscenity at the other man and threw a pillow at him. "I'm a sight prettier than you, Duke."

Derringer chuckled. "Have you need of Bruiser's help dressing? Or have you finally learned how to manage without your arm?"

"I can manage."

The duke nodded and made his way to the door. As he grasped the handle, he paused, his face to the thick wood before him. "I am pleased you survived," he told the door, his voice floating back to the man on the bed. Then he was gone.

Chapter Nine

When Gabriel emerged from his chamber, he was dressed as much as he could manage without a valet—or wife—to assist him. Worn breeches, worn hessians, a linen shirt yellowed with age, a simple blue neckerchief, and a dark blue waistcoat was as presentable as he could get. It might not be the most polite way in which to see his hostess, but Gabriel thought the duchess would forgive his lapse, under the circumstances. Derringer would probably loan him some better clothes, but Gabriel would rather wear his own worn things than the duke's morbid choices.

He stepped down the corridor, intent on going to the drawing room. It was as his foot settled on the stair that something odd struck him. He returned to his chamber.

The bag that had traveled with him and Hélène from France lay on a chair by the bed. He snatched it up and emptied it on the bed. Very little fell out. He wore his second set of clothes, so all that remained in the bag was his last clean shirt and a few keepsakes Hélène had thought to pack.

Nothing of hers fell out.

Desolation swept over him. She was gone. Not up and about, exploring a city she'd never seen or foraging for food in the gray dawn. Her things were gone. Everything.

Except the one thing he'd managed to buy for her, a few months after they'd married. A small pendant, nothing more than a pearl and a bit of blue glass with some cheap silver chain to hold it about her slim throat, glittered up at him in the shaft of sunlight that lay across the bed.

He'd spent little money on the silly little bauble, not even considering the fact that the money he spent was money his wife earned running her tavern. He barely acknowledged the cost at the time but he remembered the way she flinched when he told her. The amount of money he'd thought negligible meant far more to a woman who had to keep account of every franc earned and spent. She'd taken it, thanked him, and fretted over the accounts for weeks after.

He stared at the thing, almost as if doing so would conjure the woman to his side. How could she leave him, now, right after he found his family, his past?

Gabriel snatched up the pendant, gripping it in his fist with the intention of hurling it across the room. He barely felt the small pearl against his palm, yet it seemed warm, as if it had only just left Hélène's silken throat.

Opening his fingers, the pendant slid out, dangling before his eyes. She'd loved the thing, despite the cost. He couldn't begin to understand why. It was worthless compared to what he was used to, yet she wore it always. If she feared its loss, she kept it tucked away in the special pocket she'd sewn into all her gowns long before he met her.

"Are you lost?"

Gabriel didn't turn at his brother's voice. "Yes," he muttered, so low he didn't know if the duke heard him. He didn't care.

As he turned, he held up the necklace for his brother's inspection. "My wife has left me." He met Derringer's eyes defiantly. "I am not what she wants, it seems."

The duke, miserable bounder that he was, laughed. He strode forward and clapped Gabriel on the shoulder. "I know she wants you, little brother. After last night, no one in the square is left with any doubt of that."

Unaccountably, Gabriel felt a blush steal up his cheeks. He'd never blushed in his life that he could recall. He stifled it, shoving the pendant in the duke's face. "Put this on me."

One black brow lifted. "Not really your style, is it?"

Gabriel snorted a laugh, not having expected that particular response. "No, it's not. I care not. I mean to have it on me when I find her."

"You will look for her?"

Gabriel gave him a blank stare. "It is what St. Clairs do."

That reminder brought forth a scowl from the duke. "I saw you die, Gabe. Blood coating your chest, the life leaving your eyes. They threw you overboard." He released a frustrated growl. "I saw you die."

"I was not accusing you of anything, Hart, I swear," he hastened to assure him. "You looked for me and found me once. It was more than I deserved. Hélène returned me here, believing this to be my home."

"Is it not?"

"My home is with her, wherever that may be."

The certainty of his words shocked him. He'd thought the return of his memory would bring back every old emotion, every old desire. And seeing Michaella married was certainly jarring, sending him down a path of memories that were sweet and full of yearning. The kind of emotions one experienced when in the throws of calf love.

If only he'd realized such sooner.

"Will you help me, or must I ask Merri?"

"My wife will not be able to see through her tears," Derringer grumbled, taking the chain and working the clasp. He swiftly hooked it around Gabriel's neck. "You should find a longer chain, one that fits over your head," he muttered.

Gabriel shrugged. "This one fits over Hélène's head."

"So now what?"

That was the question. And the most frightening thing of all occurred to Gabriel in that moment. He had no idea where to even start looking. Hélène was a resourceful woman, used to making her own way, using whatever means necessary to make sure she survived.

He'd witnessed that resourcefulness firsthand. His first weeks in Hélène's tavern, he'd seen her cajole, tease, and threaten patrons into proper behavior in her establishment. And once, she'd seduced a creditor in lieu of payment for a bill. He'd thought little of it at the time, though it saddened him to see that she was in such circumstances.

An ache started in his arm, the one he no longer had, thus he ignored the sensation. It only ached when he felt the intensity of a situation he couldn't control, a problem with no foreseeable solution.

No time like the present.

Gathering his resolve, he tucked the pendant more securely beneath his neckcloth and addressed the duke. "Will you help me find her?"

Derringer smiled, the old, mischief-laden grin that Gabriel remembered from their youth. "We'll find your wife, brother. But first," he warned, throwing his arm across Gabriel's shoulders, "you must endure my wife's scolding."

Chapter Ten

The Duchess of Derringer did not disappoint. Gabriel endured tears, followed by a blistering scold, followed by more tears, which culminated in a rather brazen display of emotion that even Derringer hadn't expected. Leandra threw her arms around Gabriel and hugged him tight, as if by doing so would erase the years they'd had without him. By the time she released him, Gabriel's own eyes were moist.

"I've missed you, Merri," Gabriel assured her.

"Then why did you not return?"

Her question was so simple. But the answer was less so. "I did not remember. Anything," he admitted. He glanced toward the clock on the mantle. It was half gone ten and he knew not how many hours Hélène had been absent before he woke. "Hélène is the only reason I am here at all."

At the mention of Hélène, Leandra colored up, her face

the brightest red Gabriel had ever beheld on a human. He frowned, unsure what he'd said or done to cause the reaction.

Derringer laughed. "My wife retains much of her innocence," he mused, shooting a teasing glance in her direction, "despite my best efforts to...corrupt her."

"Hart!" she breathed, the red in her cheeks deepening even more. Forcing a serene expression that was belied by the color her face bore, she turned back to Gabriel. "Forgive him and me, my lord," she said, casting a warning glance at the duke. That man cocked a dark brow at her but said nothing. Her hazel eyes settled again on Gabriel. "Hart talked such nonsense when we returned from Michaella's wedding breakfast and realized you were here with...your wife. Hart insisted Bruiser had misheard. I...hoped otherwise."

"Why?"

Leandra's jaw dropped. "Why?"

"Yes," Gabriel repeated, "why did you hope such a thing?"

She shot a look at the duke but that man only settled back in his chair, as if to say she was on her own, rude man that he was. Gabriel's eyes never left the duchess, truly curious as to her answer.

Leandra stared, clearly flummoxed. Then, eyes narrowing, lips thinning, she took a stab in the dark. "You are as bad as him, my lord. I will not be drawn into such an indelicate conversation."

"You are in trouble, Gabe," Derringer inserted with an impish twinkle. "She's begun 'my lording' you."

Gabriel grinned. "My apologies, Merri. That was ill done of me."

Leandra never stayed mad for long. She smiled, clasping Gabriel's arm and giving it a little shake. "Now when will your wife be joining us? I am eager to meet her."

"I imagine she will be delighted to make your acquaintance, Merri," Gabriel assured her, gently disengaging himself from her, "just as soon as we find her."

"Find her? Is she not asleep?" Worry clouded her eyes, but it was nothing to the worry clouding Gabriel's.

"The bird has flown," Derringer informed her, his tone lacking anything but calm observation.

"Why?"

Gabriel scowled, dropping his lanky form into a chair despite the fact that the duchess still stood. "I know not. I woke to find her gone."

Leandra sat, clearly uncaring of her companion's bad manners. "What happened last night to make her leave?"

Gabriel and Derringer just stared at her. She stared back until her words sank in. Blushing profusely, she snapped, "Before or after, you abominable man! Clearly, something happened."

"We saw Michaella at the church."

"You did?" She reached forward to squeeze his hand.

"I'm so sorry, Gabriel."

He shook her off, unwilling to entertain the guilt that rose up in him.

Leandra frowned at his action but shook her head at her frowning husband. "Did you remember her? But you must have. Did your wife know her? Who she was, I mean?"

"Hélène said she knew who I was. I do not know how long she knew or how she knew, but..." He shrugged, the ache in his shoulder growing to the point that he rolled it, as if the action would do anything to lessen a phantom pain. "She suspected there was a woman. Very little escapes Hélène's perception. She said the pieces fell into place for her, and that they would for me too."

Leandra nodded. "Where do we start looking?"

"I haven't a clue," he admitted on a frustrated sigh. "She is adept at disappearing, hiding, finding a way to survive alone." His jaw clenched, his next words forced out. "She doesn't need anyone. She doesn't need me."

"She loves you. All we need do is find her and convince her you love her too."

The stars in Leandra's eyes revealed that deep down, she was a romantic creature who refused to believe anyone else incapable of finding love. As such, she'd not understand how Gabriel could marry a woman he didn't love, and who didn't love him.

He opened his mouth to refute her erroneous assumption but something held his tongue.

Derringer's voice broke in. "Logically, would she not seek a way to return to France, to her tavern?" He glanced away from the penknife he fiddled with, his black gaze landing on Gabriel.

"She cannot return to France." He hesitated only briefly before informing them what precipitated their flight to England. As they fired questions at him in response, his mind focused on the one thing he'd failed to remember, the one thing he'd not noticed was missing.

"The brooch," he breathed. "She took the brooch. If she sells that, she can buy passage anywhere."

"What brooch?"

"The men who sought to rob Hélène searched for something. She found it. A brooch covered in blue diamonds." He held up his fist. "This big."

Derringer's brow furrowed. "Describe it." He nodded as Gabriel described the bauble. "Good. A bit of jewelry that distinctive would not be easily sold. Would she think to break it apart, sell it bit by bit?"

"I do not know. She might."

Leandra stood. "Well then, gentlemen, is it not time we sought her out in the most obvious places?" Both men stared at her from their seated positions, identical blank stares of incomprehension. She released an exasperated breath, clearly put out with both of them. "The pawns, my loves. You should split up, each paying a call on the various shops in London who would pay good money for pieces of such a fancy brooch."

Chapter Eleven

Ah, men. Hélène sat on the front step of the pawnbroker's, her fingers wrapped around the brooch she'd found. She'd forgotten about the thing in all the upheaval of realizing her husband's love would never be hers, not while he clung to the perfect memory of his perfect bride. The brooch winked up at her, the answer to a prayer she'd not hoped to have answered.

She studied the bauble. There had been a visitor to the tavern once, long before Hélène had found Gabriel, a lady fleeing her tyrant of a husband. Clasping the edges of the lady's light cloak, the brooch had blinked in the many candles from the chandelier. Hélène greeted her, sensing the woman's tension from across the room.

"Ah! Yes, I need a room, woman. Immediately."

Hélène felt a thrum of annoyance at the lady's condescending tone. But she dipped her head, and made sure the woman was as comfortable as could be expected.

That night, Hélène heard a commotion. She slid from her bed, careful not to jar her husband awake. The window was open, allowing any breath of air to dissipate the abominable heat. A shout, a curse, and the neighing of a horse sent Hélène to the window. She saw the lady shoved into a carriage and a man climb in after her. The woman's cloak was gone.

Hélène found the garment the following day when she entered the room to clean. The brooch was still attached, a brief note pinned between it and the heavy cloth.

Many thanks for your kindness.

She'd secreted it away, touched and apprehensive, forgetting all about it in time. Her mind hadn't pondered the thing for years, only returning with the sudden appearance of the lady's husband. It had taken him years to pry the information from his wife and Hélène shuddered to think what the woman must have endured.

The lady was free now, if she still lived. Hélène pondered the wisdom of seeking her out, returning the brooch, and somehow letting her know that her husband would not be returning to England's shores.

She shook her head on the thought. It was best to leave well enough alone. She could not explain how she knew he'd expired and if she said anything, Gabriel's efforts in disposing of the bodies would be for naught.

Opening her fingers, just a bit, Hélène watched the sun

twinkle on the diamonds. She knew little of jewels, but she suspected the brooch was real and very valuable. She also assumed it was well-known. There were too many diamonds, most of them blue, in too specific a pattern, for it to be anything but specially made for a special lady.

A sigh rattled up from deep within as her fingers again concealed the brooch. She could pull it apart, sell a diamond here and there, make her way somewhere, anywhere else. But she didn't, plagued by the unshakable belief that the bauble meant something to someone once. It was a silly, romantic notion without a shred of practicality, a notion she hated, but it remained something she could not dismiss.

So she just sat there, ignored by the people who strolled by and those who entered and left the small shop, wondering what to do with the thing. It was of value to someone, she was sure, even if the lady who'd once owned it no longer lived.

How she wished for the return of her own cheap bauble. Gabriel's thoughtful, if imprudent, gift had touched her in a way nothing ever had. She nearly wept leaving it behind, but she knew it was the only way Gabriel would believe her seriousness.

Standing, she took up her bundle of belongings and stepped away, her attention on her thoughts instead of her surroundings. As she turned down an alley, deciding she'd have to find another way, she failed to note a pair of near-identical men enter the pawnbroker's.

"Describe your lady wife," Derringer ordered as Gabriel stepped toward the pawnbroker's establishment.

"Red hair, blue eyes, the look of a woman who doesn't seem to care what happens around her but misses nothing. French."

Derringer snorted, his eyes locking on Gabriel. "French? She looks French?"

Gabriel shrugged but chose not to elaborate. "Why?"

Years in the war, constantly looking over his shoulder, made Gabriel a bit more observant than most. But his brother, Lord Heartless, put him to shame with his perspicacity. With no response from the duke, Gabriel entered the pawn's. Derringer didn't follow, instead darting down a nearby alley. When Gabriel turned, he found himself face to face with an angry redhead.

"I found something of yours," Derringer drawled.

Hélène rewarded Derringer with an elbow in his ribs, forceful enough that the duke released her. "I am no one's possession," she warned him, her steady gaze never wavering.

Derringer's dark eyebrows shot upward. "Oh, Brother, I like her. Can we keep her?"

Gabriel's eyes threatened to roll, an affectation he despised. Quelling the urge, as well as the urge to use his fist to wipe the smile from the duke's face, Gabriel grasped Hélène's arm and pulled her out of the pawn's entrance and back into the alley. Once there, he released her, reached up and yanked the necklace from around his neck. "You forgot something. Pawning this won't bring you much, but it might help you forget."

"I would never do that," she sighed, her fingers wrapping around the tiny gem. "It is too valuable."

Gabriel's heart stuttered. "Why is that? You place much importance on a bauble given to you by a man you do not care to stay with."

She struck his chest. "I was never the dishonest one, Gabriel St. Clair! I was open about my feelings from the start. You clung to your precious ghost, your perfect English lady!"

"You couldn't have known that! I didn't know that!"

She threw her hands into the air and launched into rapid French, the tone indicating her frustrated displeasure even if neither man beside her could quite follow her words.

When she paused for breath, the duke broke in. "You both need to stubble it," he mused. "Marriage has taught me many things and public airing of one's grievances is not good for a union. I tried that once and slept alone for a week."

Gabriel and Hélène turned as one to stare at him, mouths hanging open at his statement. He smiled, saying nothing more, and hailed a hackney.

"Oh good, you found her," Lady Derringer said by way of greeting. She sailed forward, a plump woman clothed in a simple style, her bright hazel eyes relieved and welcoming.

Hélène didn't know how to react. A duchess, perhaps a bit less Grand Dame than Hélène expected, but still with an air of confidence that only came with the security of a title, money, and power, stood before her, clearly relieved to know she was safe. Finding herself, for once, with nothing to say, she only stared.

"What did you do to her?" Lady Derringer demanded. "She cannot even speak." She sailed forward, grasped Hélène's arm, and led her to a chair. "Sit, dear, and catch your breath. These buffoons shall go and see if Bruiser can prepare tea and leave us in peace for several minutes—twenty," she emphasized with a darkling glance at her husband, "and we shall have a comfortable coze."

Stated so adamantly, Hélène could do nothing but obey, allowing her body to gracefully fall into the indicated chair. The gentlemen, twin expressions on faces that no longer boasted identical appearances, bowed and departed. Gabriel hesitated at the door, his glance straying to Hélène's. He opened his mouth to speak, took a step in her direction, but Lady Derringer forestalled whatever he'd planned to say.

She stood, crossing the room so quickly that Hélène

blinked. She couldn't hear what was said but the duchess made it clear to Gabriel that he needed to leave.

Hélène had never been so discomposed in her life. She'd always done what she had to, when she had to. No one took care of her, made sure she was all right. No one told her what to do or how to do it. It was always her, alone, even in her previous marriage.

Now, with her first husband dead and her second husband about to leave her for his real life, his true family, she was reminded of that. She was the only one she could rely on, she was the one in control, and it was up to her to determine where her life went from that moment.

Pushing to her feet before the duchess could force Gabriel out the door, she clasped her hands before her, unsure at the odd feeling of nervousness that assailed her. "Your grace?"

Lady Derringer turned away from Gabriel. "Please, call me Leandra."

Hélène forced a smile at the generosity of her grace's request. It wasn't often a tavern owner was on such familiar terms with a member of the nobility. Especially English nobility. It was something she'd never looked to gain in her life and certainly something she could live without.

Lifting her chin a notch, she said, "Very well. Leandra. May I have a word with...my husband?"

Leandra blinked. "Certainly. Forgive my intrusion." The smile she offered was genuine, though her words implied a certain amount of hurt at Hélène's request. She dipped her head and retreated, closing the door softly behind her.

Gabriel didn't move. "You acknowledge I'm your husband."

Hélène nodded. "Of course. There's no denying that, I think."

"Does that not give me the right to decide whether or not I stay with you?"

Her heart slammed into her throat. "And what have you decided, *chéri?*"

Part of her wanted to tell him that she loved him, that she wanted him to choose her. But everything in her rebelled. How could she put herself out there, reveal just how lost she was? If he agreed with her, that he was better off in England, with his English family and English money, she would return to France, missing a part of herself but confident she would recover and thrive. Alone.

That thought sent deep melancholy spiraling through her. But with it came her usual sense of *joie de vivre*. Assuming the air of a woman who cared little about the outcome of this particular meeting, she waited for his response.

"I have decided to stay here. In England."

His casually uttered words produced no reaction in his wife. Gabriel cursed and threw his hat in the corner. Her little wall was firmly in place.

"It is best, I think," she said as if commenting on the

weather. "I shall leave for France immediately."

"We both know you can't return to France. There's that little matter of murder."

"It wasn't murder. He'd have killed you."

"How to define what happened is not the problem. Why you think you can return to France at all is."

"Then I will make a life for myself here."

The way she said it, with a hint of scorn on the word *here*, jerked a laugh from Gabriel's throat. "Indeed?"

She raised her chin, her stubborn jaw clenching as her beautiful eyes flashed with indignation. "What amuses you in that?"

"If you can stay in England, why not stay with me?"

His question did what nothing else had. It caught her off guard. But she recovered quickly, shaking off her surprise. "It would not do. You must stay here and I cannot tolerate your English nobility."

"Then I will stay with you. To hell with my English nobility."

It was her turn to laugh but the edge of bitterness was impossible to miss. "It is best for you right here, *chéri*."

Anger flared at her patronizing tone. Stalking to her side, he asked, "What is it about me that makes you think I need a mother, Hélène? What makes you coddle me, protect me, think I need someone telling me what's best? Is it the arm? Does that make me weak?"

"Don't be a fool!" She slapped his chest, but didn't

remove her hand, her fingers clenching in his shirtfront. "You need a wife who can bear you many heirs. I am not that woman."

"What makes you think that?"

"I lost another child, Gabriel. Just before we left France. I am not meant to be a mother, it seems." Tears shivered on the words, but she choked them back, unwilling to let them fall and reveal just how upset she was at the thought.

"You cannot know that," Gabriel soothed, his fingers brushing the red curls on her forehead. "I grieve for the child as I grieve for all the others, but that doesn't mean you will never be a mother." She started to protest but he interrupted with, "And even if you should never bear a child, it wouldn't matter to me."

"Don't be a fool," she repeated.

"I can't help but be so," he said, sliding his arm around her, "when you are near."

Hardly daring to breathe for fear he'd step away, laugh off his words, she whispered, "Then why do you pine for her?"

"You silly creature! I do not pine for her. I barely knew her. I loved the idea of her, the idea of the perfect, tame life she offered." He gave her a shake. "I don't love her, Hélène. It's always been you."

"Then why are we here, chasing the phantoms of your past?"

"I didn't know if she was my wife. I had to know. Surely

you understand that?" He leaned away. "And are you not the one who insisted we take this journey? Were it up to me, we'd have stayed in France, safe from my past and the ghosts I needn't have ever remembered."

Hélène heard the pain in his voice. It was more than discovering the woman he'd once loved had married another. It was remembering what led up to his arrival in France, his injuries, and the betrayal by a man he'd believed to be his brother. She'd pushed him into remembering, not for his own wellbeing, but for selfish reasons of her own. She refused to share him with a phantom.

"I am sorry," she whispered. "I brought this on. I should have left well enough alone."

"Perhaps you should have," he said, but he didn't push her away. He drew her closer, resting his head on hers. "But if you had left well enough alone, I'd never have remembered Hart, and he's been my best friend since we were in short coats."

"And he's your real brother, *chéri*. You needn't fret over the acts of that other man."

"Just so."

"Perhaps, if you are well-behaved, I will consider staying with you," she offered, smiling into his neckcloth.

He chuckled. "You don't like me well-behaved."

Her laughter rumbled through him. She lifted her head. "You are the very best lord I've ever known."

Gabriel stared down at her, seeing so much more in her eyes than she revealed with her words. His grin stretched. "Ah, my heart belongs to you, too, my lady."

Her arrested expression drew another laugh from him. "You did not consider that, did you, my love? Marriage to me means you are a lady. So I guess the real question is, do you wish to stay with me?"

And that was the question. It was never about Gabriel's decision. It was always with Hélène. Could she countenance a life lived amongst the English elite, moving about the rich and entitled as if she belonged?

Her response, when it came, was in an exaggerated upper class English accent that Gabriel found as a endearing as it was appalling.

"Why yes, my lord, I do believe I shall stay with you."

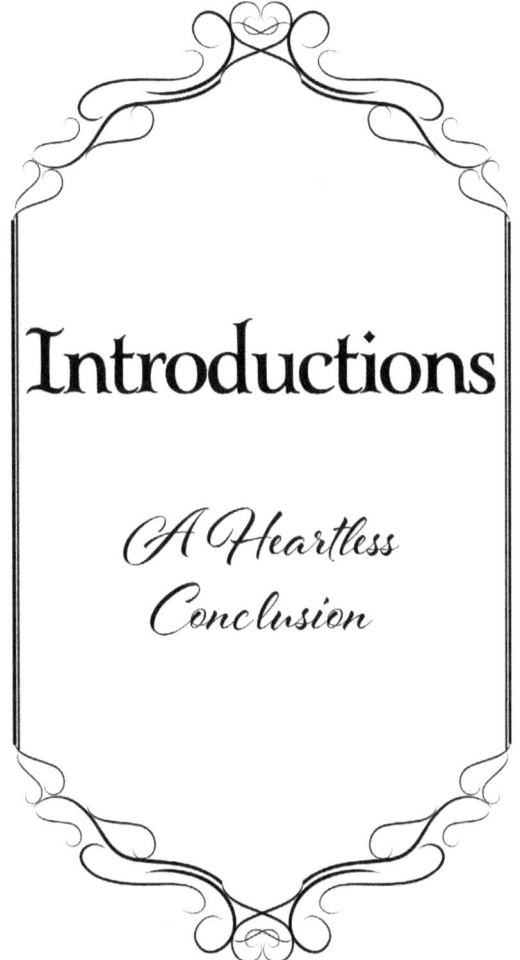

Introductions

A Heartless
Conclusion

Chapter One

England 1824

"Lord and Lady Gabriel St. Clair!"

Michaella's head whipped up at the majordomo's stentorian announcement. "Gabe?" slipped from her lips just before those very lips were ruthlessly pressed against another pair of lips.

"My love," Rhys mused between kisses to her neck and face, "calling out...another man's name...whilst making love to...your husband...is very bad form." He renewed his assault on her lips, giving her no opportunity to respond, if a coherent response was something she could even manage at the moment. His hands pulled her close, fingers splayed across her back. "Very...bad...form."

Summoning an inhuman amount of control, Michaella pulled away, far enough to regard her husband's smiling countenance. "Seducing one's wife"—she placed a hand over his mouth as he leaned in to continue said seduction —"in an alcove...in the middle of the day...across from the drawing room...no less...is most improper."

"Your speech would have been far more effective had you kissed me with each pause, my love," Rhys mused, allowing her just a touch more distance, though he didn't actually release her.

She smiled. "Perhaps, but how much of it would you have remembered after?"

He twined his fingers with hers, staring down at the linked appendages. "This is the first moment I've had alone with you in days." He bestowed his most earnest expression on her, adding just a touch of pathetic entreaty.

She scowled at his emotional appeal, or tried to. "Stealing into an alcove is your way to remedy that?" She wanted to ask him why he didn't simply enter her bedchamber on any of the past few nights. She wanted to ask him why he chose to *sleep* in his own chamber, for that matter. But good breeding would not allow her to ask such an indelicate question.

Instead, she allowed him to seduce her in a most inappropriate place, where any one of their guests might happen upon them, causing quite the countryside scandal. And as she pondered the possible ramifications, his hand slid down her shoulder, passing ever so lightly over her breast and on down to curl around her corseted ribs. Her breath caught as she vividly remembered the feel of his hands on her skin instead of hampered by several layers of sensible silk and whalebone.

And no guests constantly underfoot.

"Darling, your every waking moment since we left London has been filled with planning and family and servants," Rhys patiently explained, trailing kisses over her cheeks and neck. Michaella's heart kicked up a beat, her fingers clenching in the rough cloth of Rhys' jacket. "I saw a moment and took advantage."

And what he meant by that was he saw her in the foyer, greeting a newly arrived guest, and spirited her into the curtained alcove. Concerned that something had gone horribly wrong with one of the male guests at this, her very first house party, she'd followed with nothing more than a truncated "Please excuse—" directed at the new arrivals.

She could barely contain her shock when, instead of speaking, her very proper and gentlemanly husband pulled her into his arms and kissed her like a starving man. Too shocked to protest and—admittedly—pleasantly surprised, he'd managed to distract her quite well for several minutes.

Until Huxley's voice broke through the sensual haze, intoning a name she'd not heard in months, the name of a man she'd not *seen* in years. How was it possible that he chose to attend her house party?

The summer months blazed hot, making London unpleasant. When Rhys suggested a house party in the country, Michaella agreed, having just received the news of Gabriel's survival. She needed time away, time to think, to come to terms with her love for her husband and the natural feelings she still harbored for a man she'd thought long dead. It wasn't everyday a lady received such news.

And now he was in her home. Why?

Pushing against Rhys' shoulders, she managed to steal a moment of sanity. "Rhys?" she gasped.

"Darling?" He pressed his lips to the tempting bit of flesh he'd just exposed with a few flicks of his clever fingers, completely undeterred by her withdrawal.

"Rhys!"

He lifted his head. "My love?"

"We must go to the drawing room."

Rhys sighed. "Must we, my love? I find your company much more...stimulating"—he grinned wickedly, white teeth flashing in the dim glow surrounding them—"than that of the bores in the drawing room."

Michaella's eyes narrowed even as heat stole up her throat. "You spend far too much time in Hart's company, I think. His bad manners are infectious, a disease."

His grin widened at her accusation, the same mirthful grin she'd learned early on was something uniquely him, the grin that used his charming dimple to full advantage.

The smile that made Michaella's upset melt away and

her heart skip a beat.

Her body swayed toward him, only a very small part of her brain shouting warnings that she was succumbing to his wiles and would soon allow him to have his way with her, right there in the alcove.

For shame!

Rhys jerked back, an unlovely shade of pink coloring his high cheekbones in the sudden flare of light invading their small space. His gaze slid over her shoulder and, with a sinking in the pit of her stomach, she realized they were not alone. The words she'd thought only in her head had actually been spoken aloud and not by her.

She turned, slowly. "Hart," she greeted, pulling the sleeve of her gown back up on her shoulder and straightening her rumpled skirts. "So lovely of you to join us."

"I might believe you if you didn't glare in such a becoming manner," the Duke of Derringer mused, grinning in such a way that Michaella longed to slap him for his impertinence. "You are looking lovely, as always." He craned his neck, peeking back over his shoulder at someone Michaella couldn't see due to his tall form blocking the view. "My darling bride has seen me and her natural curiosity draws her hither." He gestured at Michaella's chest. "I suggest you make yourself presentable." With a cheeky grin, he added in his very best imitation of a subservient page, "Iffin' it please you, mum?"

If embarrassment hadn't immediately flared at his observation—the top six buttons of her sensible morning dress were undone, revealing her chemise and a generous expanse of creamy skin!—Michaella would have slapped the infuriating duke. Instead, she spun about, nearly slamming into her oddly silent husband.

"Allow me," he offered, doing up the buttons in only a few moments. "Duke, we will join the company presently."

Derringer snapped a smart bow, his scarred visage still boasting the grin that made Michaella want to slap him. He disappeared, dropping the curtain and allowing them the dimness they'd so recently enjoyed.

And with his exit came the return of Michaella's unease. In her drawing room was the gentleman she once loved and promised to marry.

The man she'd believed to be dead until a few months ago.

Pain knotted her stomach, lightness filling her head. "I am unwell." Reaching out, she clasped Rhys' arm just as darkness claimed her.

A man would have to be a saint to feel nothing when his wife faints at the mere *idea* of seeing her former love.

"I'm not a bloody saint," Rhys muttered as he hefted his bride over his shoulder like a sack of potatoes. Most undignified, he knew, but he saw little help for it. With his bad leg, he could not cradle her in his arms. He needed one hand to hold his cane. And summoning a servant for assistance would only serve to make her malady public knowledge, bringing humiliation down on both their heads.

The house party was his idea, one he was coming to deeply regret. The place crawled with friends and family, many Rhys had never met before this gathering, some he wished he never had. Michaella's family wasn't one he'd choose to associate with, other than the Derringers, and he'd yet to meet her brother, the brother who'd had a hand in trying to kill Derringer and Gabriel St. Clair. He suspected he'd not care for the man above half.

But that would never be an issue, considering Derringer would kill the blighter if he dared set foot on England's shores again.

A new problem occurred to Rhys as he carefully turned. There were kids everywhere, more than he'd happened to see in one place in the entirety of his life. How could he possibly remove her from the alcove and into his study, sight unseen?

Oh well. He'd simply have to explain then, and hope for the best possible result. He'd have shrugged at the futility of it all if his charming bride wasn't currently slung over his shoulder. Peeking between the alcove's curtains, Rhys at least attempted to determine he'd not be seen. Then he slipped away into the back of the manor.

Chapter Two

Gabriel St. Clair sat in the drawing room wondering if he'd lost his mind. Just what the devil was he doing, attending a house party hosted by the husband of the woman he once loved and promised to marry, and attended by half the people in existence he'd have paid a great deal of money to avoid? Was he insane?

Which led to the question as to why they'd been invited in the first place, and why his beautiful wife insisted on attending.

Barely able to sit still, he rose, bowing to Hélène. "My apologies, my love, but I must excuse myself." He barely acknowledged the two women flanking her—Michaella's insufferable mother, the Dowager Countess of Harwood, and Michaella's painfully mousy sister, Lady Schuster. He supposed he should be thankful his own unbearable relatives were absent from this particular party.

Hélène stared up at him, brows raised in patent disbelief at his abandonment. "Very well, my lord," she allowed, only the slightest derogatory emphasis on *my lord*. Gabriel was the only one who'd notice. "I shall wait here for you, *oui*?"

His relief at her ready capitulation knew no bounds. He smiled, excused himself to the party in general and exited the chamber. A movement from the back caught his eye, drawing it there. A man stumbled out of sight, the body of a woman draped over his shoulder. He'd have laughed if he didn't know immediately who they were.

Gabriel might not have officially met Rhys Wainwright, but that didn't mean he wasn't able to recognize him at a glance. He'd heard much of the man, and Derringer had made sure to point him out once. The man's limp, how he used a cane to steady his gait rather than as an affectation, the very manner in which he struggled over his burden, all told Gabriel his host was in a pinch. But who did he carry with such painstaking care? Was it Michaella?

Curiosity was ever Gabriel's failing and he couldn't resist the urge to follow Mr. Wainwright now. He didn't bother sneaking; he simply strolled as if he had every right to follow them into the small study located in the furthest recesses of the house, away from the noise of everyday life.

He stood in the door, watching Rhys as that man stood before the large, sturdy sofa, frowning. It dawned on Gabriel that his host was in a quandary, trying to determine how to relieve himself of his burden with as much dignity as he could.

"Considering you carted her in here over your shoulder," Gabriel mused, "do you not think dignity is already lost?"

Rhys spun, nearly upsetting himself in his haste to see who addressed him so informally. "Lord Gabriel!" He frowned up at the ceiling. "Would it be too much to ask...?"

The laugh Gabriel released startled Rhys. "I can be of some assistance, I'm sure," he said, waving his one arm at his host.

Rhys snorted. "I am sure with your one good arm and my one good leg, we can manage."

Gabriel grinned, liking his host far more than he expected. "I shall keep you from falling over, shall I, whilst you place her upon the sofa?"

"Very well," Rhys acquiesced, though Gabriel could tell he wasn't too keen on the idea of needing help at all. But when one suffered an injury that changed one's life, one must adapt or die. Adaptation sometimes meant asking for help on far more occasions than one was comfortable with.

Rhys allowed his cane to fall against the sofa and Gabriel readied himself in case the other gentleman needed a steadying hand as he attempted to gently release his burden rather than dump her like a sack of grain. But Rhys acquitted himself well, barely tottering as he allowed Michaella to slide down into his arms and leaned forward to place her on the sofa. Much weight was placed on his injured limb and Gabriel, watching as closely as he was, saw the wince of pain the other man tried to conceal.

As he let Michaella go, Rhys staggered, dropping her the last few inches. Gabriel jumped forward but Rhys steadied, waving him away.

Gabriel retrieved Rhys' cane and held it out. "Well done."

"Thank you." He glanced around the study and back at his guest. "Is there something I can help you with?"

"'Unfailingly polite.' I heard that about you."

Rhys' brows rose. "Indeed?"

"There were other things mentioned, but I dismissed them as feminine prattle." He grinned again, almost hoping Rhys would ask. It was his brother Derringer coming out in him, he knew, something that happened more and more as he spent more time with him, but something he had little desire to eradicate from his being.

Rhys said nothing more about it, however. He shrugged and pushed Michaella's legs over so he could sit beside her. Looking up, he offered, "By all means, be seated, if you wish."

Gabriel glanced away, his gaze settling on Michaella, finally. It was the first he'd seen her since his arrival. Her features were the same as he remembered, serene, beautiful, utterly calming in the most turbulent of storms. There was a new peace, however, one that came with finding happiness and contentment with another. She'd moved on, forgotten all about him. How he could tell this while she lay unconscious was a mystery, one that made him distinctly uncomfortable.

"No. Thank you. I merely wished to ascertain whether or not Mi—ssus Wainwright was well." He paused, hoping Rhys hadn't noticed his informal slip over Michaella's name. "Seeing her thus drew my concern," he explained, waving his hand in her direction.

"She but came over faint." Rhys paused, as if daring Gabriel to comment. "The heat."

"Of course."

Gabriel glanced at her one last time before dismissing himself. He had no desire to be present when Michaella regained her wits. He'd abandoned her and despite her having found happiness in the meantime, he was unsure how she'd react to his presence.

What a mistake it had been to attend her house party!

Chapter Three

Michaella's great comfort was her sister. This was the usual thing, the two girls having been very close throughout their childhoods. Lady Harwood had done her best to keep them apart, even going so far as to send them to different finishing schools, but none of her machinations bore fruit. The girls remained the very best of friends.

Having Leandra with her during this latest emotional struggle was most comforting. Michaella wasn't even sure what about the situation filled her with dread. Was she really afraid seeing Gabriel again, face to face, would send her into raptures of lost love found? It sounded ridiculous. She was far too sensible a creature to even entertain such a notion.

She found Leandra in the nursery, doting upon all the youngest children who'd been brought by their parents. There were several babies present, beautiful creatures, all happy smiles and chubby arms. A few of the attending mothers were there, playing with their youngest children.

Leandra sat off to the side, her daughter Penelope in her decreasing lap. Penelope was a pretty little thing who favored her father's dark coloring. Leandra talked to the child, smiling at the little girl's answering giggles.

Michaella's stomach clenched. Her hand brushed lightly over her middle. She wanted a little one so much. She suspected she might be increasing, but she wasn't sure and wouldn't be sure for several days yet. Pushing the thoughts aside, she strode forward, greeting the other ladies who happened to be visiting their children that morning.

The older children had all gone off on some adventure accompanied by Lord Claremont and Miss Emerson. As the youngest of the actual party guests, they were very helpful caring for their younger siblings, keeping them out of the way and entertained. Michaella suspected they didn't mind being in each other's company either.

"Kaylee!" Leandra smiled at Michaella. "Have you come to see your niece? She's grown even in the short time since you'd last seen her."

"Indeed she has," Michaella agreed. She sat beside her sister and took Penelope onto her own lap, her glance straying to the other woman's greatly distended belly. She wanted to ask her so many questions but good breeding forbade mentioned such an indelicate subject.

Until Leandra sucked in a breath and pushed her hands

against her stomach.

"Merri! What ails you? Is it the child?"

Leandra waved a hand at her, dismissing the possibility. "It's too soon," she breathed.

Michaella sent a disbelieving glance her way. "Are you sure, Merri? You are much bigger than I would have thought."

Tears pooled in Leandra's eyes and trickled down her cheeks. "It is too soon! Too soon!"

Penelope set up a wailing at her mother's panicked tone, the other babies joining in one by one until the room filled with a cacophony of tiny voices, all raised in protest.

Michaella stood, handing the sobbing Penelope off to a nursery maid, while addressing another. "Call for the midwife. This baby refuses to wait." The maid rushed off, not even bothering with a curtsy. "Take the children into the schoolroom." The other maids jumped to do her bidding while the other mothers, Ladies Windhaven and Greville, rushed off to gather the things they would need to birth the baby.

Michaella knelt at her sister's feet. "Breathe, Merri, breathe. Panic will do no good."

"But Leander was too early. He died!"

And Michaella hadn't been there. She'd been so wrapped up in her own misery and guilt that she'd neglected her sister, to the point that she wasn't there for her when her tiny infant died, barely a sennight after his birth.

"This is not Leander, love, and I'm sorry for that, more than I can say." Michaella pressed Leandra's hands. "I know you are scared." She had to pause, swallowing against her own numbing fear. "But you must calm yourself, for you and the baby. Please, Merri."

Leandra took several deep breaths, her tears nothing more than silent streaks of wetness against her pale skin. Michaella breathed a little sigh of relief herself as the tension left her sister's body.

The housekeeper bustled in. "There now, yer grace, let's get you up and about, m'dear." Her smile went far in spreading a little calm over the room's occupants.

Michaella took one arm while Mrs. March took the other. They hefted Leandra to her feet, making their slow, ponderous way to her bedchamber. Once there, they found Lady Greville bustling about readying everything they'd need, with Lady Windhaven following after them with her arms full of fresh linens. Hélène entered right after her, her arms also full of linens.

"I found another to aid us," Raven, Lady Windhaven explained to the room in general. Her husky voice was oddly soothing. "Hélène was wandering the corridors alone. That simply would not do." She smiled at Hélène and moved to one side of the bed, depositing her burden on a chair.

The Frenchwoman's gaze skittered across the room, a

nervous twitch of her lips alerting Michaella that she was most uncomfortable there. She didn't have time to worry over anyone's comfort but Leandra's at the moment, however, so she and Mrs. March swiftly divested the duchess of her garments and draped her in a clean nightrail.

It was as they settled her in the large bed that Derringer burst in, the midwife on his heels.

"Merri!"

Leandra forced herself to sit up, one hand extended to her husband. "Hart! The baby—"

"Is well, Merri," Michaella insisted.

The midwife dried her freshly washed hands on a clean linen towel. "Everyone out," she ordered firmly, her gaze on the laboring mother and no one else.

Derringer, of course, balked. "I will not!"

Michaella, foreseeing much bloodshed, grasped the duke's arm. "Come, Hart. You must allow the midwife to examine her."

"I will not leave her!"

"You must. It will not do to have you here."

His gaze shifted from her to his wife. "I must stay."

Michaella didn't take no for an answer. She simply took his arm, nodded at Hélène to take his other, and they led him from the chamber. He hesitated so the other ladies took up the rear, each putting a hand in his back and urging him from the room.

Michaella glanced over her shoulder. The last thing she

saw as the door closed was the midwife holding Leandra's hand, her soothing voice calming the mother-to-be. Michaella breathed a sigh of relief, knowing her sister was in good hands.

As word swiftly spread of the duchess' lying-in, the drawing room filled with the party guests, all eager to hear how she fared. The gentlemen stayed away, though Rhys and Gabriel stepped in and tried to take Derringer away with them. He refused to go so Michaella shooed them off and sat next to Derringer, one hand on his arm, more to keep him from bolting to Leandra's side than to calm him. His hands hung limply between his knees, head bowed and black hair masking his features entirely from the room. She couldn't imagine what he was feeling but if it was even close to the fear she felt, she pitied him.

"I failed her once."

Michaella's heart skipped at beat at the lowly uttered words. "Hart?"

He lifted his head, only enough to meet Michaella's eyes. His hands tightened until the knuckles turned white. "Leander. I wasn't there. I thought...I thought she'd be...well. But he came early. Too early."

Michaella squeezed his arm. Tears sprang to her eyes at the raw emotion in his tone. "This isn't the same," she assured him.

"Is it not?"

"No." She couldn't explain her assurance.

The butler entered, eyes scanning the gathering, and made his way to Michaella's side. He handed her a note. She quickly read the hastily scrawled words.

Derringer's head snapped up. "What? What is it?"

Michaella considered leaving him there and speaking to the midwife herself. But one look at the pain in his eyes and she took his arm, tugging him to his feet. "Come. The midwife asked to speak with me."

They found the midwife waiting for them in the foyer, readying herself to depart.

"Mrs. Smythe?" Michaella asked, stepping forward to stop the woman. "Why do you depart?"

"Oh, milady, her grace is well," the midwife hastened to assure them. "False pains. Keep her calm, and keep her to her chamber as much as possible." She offered the duke an encouraging smile, bobbed a curtsy, and left.

Michaella turned to Derringer. He stood there, face blanked of all emotion. "False pains?" he asked, his eyes pinned to the door through which the midwife has just disappeared.

"The baby is not yet here," Michaella explained, not sure how much her brother-by-marriage understood of childbirth and its mysteries.

Derringer's gaze shifted, finally meeting hers. "Not yet?"

"No."

"This one will survive?"

Michaella smiled, wanting to offer him an unequivocal yes, wanting to believe that herself. But that decision was out of her hands. "Only God can know that. Rest easy in the knowledge that the baby will have more time to grow."

Chapter Four

A sennight passed and Michaella and Gabriel managed to avoid one another the entirety of that time. It was a conscious decision on neither of their parts, but a decision nonetheless, one that was adhered to with bitter determination.

One that left their spouses flummoxed.

Lady Gabriel St. Clair—Hélène to her intimates, few as they may be—sat in the rear garden, admiring the bees buzzing around the late summer blooms. She was alone, an odd circumstance when one attended a house party. She sat and stared, wondering why she was there and what she'd hoped to accomplish when she'd convinced her husband to attend.

She'd hoped to alleviate her own fears, she admitted with her typical inner candor. She feared Gabriel wasn't as "over" his former love as he'd claimed and Hélène wanted to prove to herself and to him that Michaella Wainwright was very much past loving him. Hélène had thought it necessary but now she saw the flaw in her own plan.

They still loved each other.

Tears threatened. Hélène never cried. She was French, not given to sentimentality, and had once owned a tavern and managed it all on her own. She needed no one in her life and though she'd found comfort in Gabriel's arms, she'd be well if he chose to walk away.

Or so she told herself.

She shook her head. She wouldn't be well and she knew it. She'd survive, true, but surviving was a far cry from well.

"Why so gloomy?"

She turned, pasting a smile on her lips for the benefit of her host. "Not gloomy, *monsieur*, merely thoughtful."

Rhys Wainwright offered her a smile, the dimple peeking out in his cheek making her smile genuinely in return. "That's all right then." He gestured to the bench upon which she sat. "May I?"

"*Oui.*" She slid over to make sure he had plenty of room. "What brings you to the garden, *monsieur* Rhys?"

He said nothing of her use of his given name. "The need to commune with nature."

The way he said it, as if it was a question, made her laugh. "Indeed? Then I invite you to do so. The bees, there, are most industrious."

He chuckled. "Thank you."

Silence fell between them, a comfortable one that neither found the need to break. Until one of those industrious bees decided to examine the artificial flower that adorned Hélène's very smart bonnet. She jumped, swatting at the thing. Rhys attempted to shoo it away as well but their efforts were for naught. It swooped down, embedding its stinger deep in Hélène's tender flesh.

Her eyes widened. "*Merde.*"

Rhys' eyes widened. "Colorful."

Hélène didn't smile, her mind entirely absorbed in the pain radiating from her neck. She reached up and fingered the wound. How could a simple bee sting hurt so much? Hot, stabbing pain, like a fire-kissed blade, pierced her flesh. It was unreal.

Eyes meeting Rhys' again, she breathed, "I am lost," in true, melodramatic fashion.

Rhys did not smile. "Nonsense. It's a mere bee sting. Painful, but you will recover." He studied her upturned face. Hélène didn't know what he looked for but she could only stare back, aware of burning pain and little else. "How is it you've never before experienced a bee sting?"

She shrugged but immediately regretted the action. Teeth clenched, she said, "I have not. I do not know how I've avoided it but I wish I had continued to do so."

He did smile then, taking her hand and giving it a comforting squeeze. "It will pass, the pain, but it might hurt for some time yet. Would you like a restorative tea, or sherry?"

"Good French brandy, I think," she said, unashamed and uncaring if he thought her request scandalous. A lady never drank such strong spirits.

"Brandy it is, then. I believe we still have the bottle Derringer presented to my bride and me on our wedding day."

"Smuggled, no doubt."

"Indeed. This is the perfect time for it, I think."

"I could not agree more, *monsieur*."

Chapter Five

Days later, Rhys found himself in the stables, saddling a horse in a blind rage. He didn't know why he hadn't realized it sooner. What a fool he was!

How had he not seen that Michaella, though claiming otherwise, was still deeply in love with Lord Gabriel St. Clair? Her avoidance of the man and unwillingness to discuss him was proof enough to convince Rhys. He refused to believe he'd never been entirely sure, that he'd always feared there might still be some feelings there, some trace amount of longing for the man she'd once promised to marry.

The chestnut mare he'd saddled balked when Rhys threw himself on. He cursed, forcing at least a semblance of calm over his tense frame, at least enough that the blasted creature would leave the stable yard without tossing him.

And to think, the blame for this situation could be laid

firmly at his own feet! He was the one to invite the St. Clairs, hoping to lay the ghost of Gabriel's and Michaella's love to rest. His plan seemed to have blown apart, right before his very eyes.

In his selfish desire, he'd also hurt Hélène, a woman as innocent as one could be. She'd married Lord Gabriel with no knowledge of his past or who he might have loved.

So why had they chosen to attend?

That particular question nagged at Rhys now and had since their arrival. A fortnight into the house party and Rhys still didn't know. He watched Michaella and he watched Gabriel. At times, he watched Hélène, curious to note the way she watched everyone as well. He attributed it to her desire not to embarrass herself or her husband amongst those who held him in the highest esteem, as well as those who did not.

But Hélène said and did things that shocked those around her. Rhys suspected she did so quite intentionally. Why, just that morning she asked Lady Harwood what scent she preferred and when receiving that lady's reply, Hélène asked her why she did not simply bathe regularly and save a fortune on purchasing scent! In one short conversation she'd managed to touch on two subjects not mentioned in polite conversation.

The Dowager's reaction had been priceless. Her face turned purple with rage, but powers of speech had been robbed from her in her shock. She'd flounced from the room like an outraged débutante.

Rhys chuckled at the memory. His mother-in-law was not his favorite person and she'd made it clear to him early on that the feeling was quite mutual.

His mirth died a quick death. It was clear Hélène didn't care a whit what the other guests thought of her. Even if it embarrassed her husband, who seemed to find nothing but amusement in her behavior.

Rhys jerked back on the reins, sending his mount into a nervous fit as she tried to regain her bearings. He soothed her with a few low words, his mind only half on the task.

What if Lady Gabriel St. Clair didn't watch those around her in an effort to avoid a *faux pas*? What if she looked for something else?

He spun the horse about, the poor creature finally thinking along the same lines as her rider. They flew back to the manor. When he arrived, he paused next to Jeb, the stablehand who'd been on hand when he'd first saddled the horse. Sliding from the animal, he came down just a bit too hard on his bad leg, the limb buckling beneath him. Jeb grasped his arm, preventing a nasty, embarrassing fall, and shoved the cane he held into Rhys' hand.

"Thank you, Jeb." Rhys hated the weakness that sometimes reared its ugly head but he'd learned to accept it and move on. He'd also learned to move with great care to prevent exactly what had almost happened. It seemed his anxiety over the state of his wife's heart was enough to ignore everything he'd learned about managing his injury.

Jeb doffed his hat. "Sir." The stablehand reached for the reins, preparatory to leading the beast back to her stall.

Regarding the heaving sides of the poor horse, Rhys frowned. "Treat her well, Jeb. I've misused her sorely, I fear."

Jeb nodded, giving the mare a pat on the neck. He led her off without another word.

The rear garden was the one place generally avoided by the other party guests. Hélène supposed the heat kept many of the ladies indoors, sitting lethargically near an open window in hopes that a breeze would brush over them, their fans becoming more than just a pretty trinket to hang from their wrists.

This lack of human presence was probably why she was attracted to the garden—despite her recent misadventure with the bee—longing for the solitude she'd once only enjoyed at her less than busy tavern.

She missed the place, the independence it entailed, but she wasn't about to admit that to anyone. She was trying to make a place for herself in England, with her husband's noble family, despite her inclination to run from the nobility and their ilk.

A step on the stone walk drew her attention. Mr. Wainwright bore down on her, eyes hard in his handsome face. She was unconcerned, allowing a moment of observation before he was upon her.

He was a handsome man, she allowed, dark hair and blue eyes, features of a hawkish cast that gave him a brooding look. But she'd seen him smile, a dimple peeking out to turn those sharp features into something quite different. Hélène's eyes traveled brazenly over his person, admiring the way his leather breeches clung to his thighs. Though one could tell he had a weakness in one leg, he was still a fine specimen of a man.

Her lips quirked. Many a maiden would have lost her...heart. Hélène certainly wouldn't have thrown him from her bed.

Before she'd met Gabriel, of course.

His cane was not for show. No, indeed, he made generous use of it, his lumbering gait suggesting his injury still pained him. Lady Michaella attracted lame ducks, it seemed, having fallen in love with one in possession of only one arm, and then marrying a cripple.

Rhys drew up beside her. His eyes suggested something angered him. He settled on the bench without invitation, looking straight ahead, both hands folded over the head of his cane. Voice low, he said, "I know why you are here."

Chapter Six

Michaella searched high and low for her husband, concerned that he seemed to have disappeared into the very mist that now lay upon the moors. The heat of the day had dissipated along with the sun's descent, leaving an odd, damp cold that soaked into one's flesh, right down to the marrow. If Rhys was out in such weather, he'd be miserable when he returned, his wound causing him much pain during such times.

Her mind and body refused to settle. She needed to find him, discover what plagued him so these past days. He'd been distant, withdrawn. It was so unlike the cheerful, playful man she'd married that her concern slipped dangerously close to outright fear. What had occurred to engender such a reaction from him?

"My lady?"

Michaella turned. Many still addressed her by her title,

though she preferred to be called Mrs. Wainwright. There was so much more to be proud of in being Rhys' wife than in being the daughter of an earl, even if she had loved her father more than many daughters in the same position.

"Miss Emerson," she greeted one of their younger guests. The pretty young woman smiled, dipping a respectful curtsy as she did so.

"I must beg your pardon, my lady," Linnet explained. "My sister is feeling poorly and I wish to attend her this evening. I am sorry we will be unable to enjoy the entertainment."

Michaella smiled though she knew the falsehood for what it was. Linnet's sister was a former actress, now married to a duke. She was quite the actress, Michaella knew from having seen the woman perform once. She must miss her former life, and the thought of attending the amateur theatrics planned for the evening was probably more than she could bear.

Or she couldn't bear the thought of the amateur part of the theatrics, Michaella mused cynically.

"Of course. I'm very sorry." She studied Linnet's face for a moment, part of her just as desperate to avoid the entertainment as Lady Windhaven. Hitting upon an idea, she offered, "Shall I sit with your sister so you may attend?"

For the briefest moment, Linnet's features lit from within. It wasn't the glow of a girl eager to attend a demonstration of amateur theatrics. Rather, it was the look of a young woman distracted by the thought of being in a particular young gentleman's company.

It had to be Deveraux, Lord Preston's son and heir. He was of an age with Linnet, in possession of blond curls, blue eyes, pretty manners, and a title. He was a catch, to be sure.

Michaella smiled, remembering that emotion well, even if it was for a man she hadn't ended up marrying.

But the look faded, replaced with a determination that was a bit startling in one so young. "I am obliged, ma'am, but it is unnecessary."

"Will Lord Windhaven be attending?"

"I do not know," Linnet admitted. "He is visiting the village tavern with the other gentlemen. I know not if they will return in time." She bobbed a curtsy and excused herself.

Michaella watched her leave. Was that where Rhys had gotten off too? What an odd turn of events.

Deciding to do a bit of matchmaking, Michaella went off to visit the Duchess of Windhaven. If she could convince that lady to allow her sister to attend the evening's entertainment, perhaps Linnet would be able to further her acquaintance with Deveraux. Of course, Michaella would first have to ascertain if the match was acceptable to the parents. With all her experience in Society, however, she saw little obstacle to the match.

Smiling despite her worry over Rhys, Michaella marched off to the guest chambers. The amateur theatrics might have been her idea, but she had no desire to attend herself. And at the moment, she didn't care that it would look odd for the hostess to be absent.

Chapter Seven

Rhys bumped into the gentleman beside him, released an unmanly giggle, and righted himself with all the dignity at his disposal, which wasn't much. Gabriel happened to be the one he jostled and that man simply shoved him back, nearly sending him into the gentleman on his other side, the heartless duke himself.

He had no idea how he must appear and little cared. He'd enjoyed his time with the other men, some of whom he'd barely known beyond a title and now he considered new friends. Lord Preston was a good sort, though his drinking took on a rather harsh edge, punctuated with complaints about his harpy wife. Derringer, Gabriel, the Duke of Windhaven, and Rhys all sat mum, having nothing to say against their spouses but unwilling to stop another man from venting his frustrations in the relative safety of men who understood even if they didn't share his opinions.

When Schuster joined in, a man Rhys found himself disliking though he was the husband of Michaella's sister, Rhys decided he'd had enough and made his way home, Derringer and Gabriel opting to accompany him while Windhaven stayed behind on some business of his own.

Rhys hadn't realized just how much he'd had to drink until he stumbled from the carriage, nearly ending with his face in fresh horse droppings. Derringer and Gabriel kept him upright, the duke's free hand holding Rhys' stick. They made their stumbling way to Rhys' chamber and deposited him at the door. Derringer, who'd somehow managed to retain his wits though he'd knocked back as many tankards as the rest of them, propped Rhys against the doorjamb, shoved Rhys' walking stick into his hand, and tapped on the door. Then, with a mocking salute in Rhys' direction, he grasped Gabriel firmly by the arm and escorted him several doors down the corridor and deposited him there.

"Gentlemen," he said, bowing, "it has been a pleasure!" He left them with a laugh.

Rhys would have reacted if his wife hadn't that moment opened the door. He glanced around. It wasn't his chamber Derringer had delivered him to, it was Michaella's.

Lady Michaella breathed a sigh of relief. "Rhys! Thank heavens. I was so worr—"

Rhys didn't allow her to finish. He dropped his cane and took the one step forward that separated them, pulling her close. He tried to kiss her but Michaella shoved at him.

"Rhys?"

"Come, love, let us adjourn to the bed and finish what we started earlier."

Michaella's nose wrinkled. "Are you drunk?"

When Rhys attempted to shrug nonchalantly, the world tilted. Michaella reached out and pulled him into the room, barely able to keep his tall frame upright. She frowned at him, the expression seeming extremely funny to his drink-clouded eyes.

His laughter abruptly ceased when his loving wife released him. He fell into a chair, a hard, upright thing that sent his insides slamming about, threatening to spill forth. "Hell, woman!"

"There is no call for such language!"

Michaella spun on her heel and left him there, his head spinning. He sucked in a breath, fought the rising bile, and tried to make sense of what just happened.

He'd gone into the village, not to drink himself stupid, but to take his mind off his own ridiculous fears. His wife might love someone else, but she would never stray. And the way Lord Gabriel spoke of his own wife would convince anyone with half a brain that he loved her. So all Rhys had to do was accept whatever crumbs Michaella was willing to give him.

At the mere thought of that, Rhys flung himself forward, reaching the chamberpot under the bed just in time.

Chapter Eight

"I thought these days long passed, *chéri*," Hélène murmured as she divested Gabriel of his boots and coat.

"What days, love?" Gabriel muttered, trying to undo the buttons of his jacket with one fumbling hand.

"The days you drink yourself into a stupor to forget her."

He said nothing in response, all his attention on the buttons that refused to be undone. Sighing, she pushed his hand away and undid them herself. Gabriel smiled, leaning in to kiss her. Hélène allowed one kiss, then pushed him back so he lay on the bed.

"Rest now, *chéri*," she admonished. "Sleep off the drink."

He grunted in response and Hélène knew he was well on his way to that state. She left him there, exiting the room in search of some unoccupied spot in the house.

The corridors were empty but for the occasional servant

bustling to this or that chamber, seeking to make all the guests comfortable. Hélène still wasn't quite used to having servants underfoot. Indeed, she quite preferred when they visited the Derringers, who eschewed the trend of having a servant for every little job. They had a handful whom they paid well. Thankfully, Gabriel took a page from his brother's book and only employed a handful as well. Hélène was sure she couldn't abide more.

She passed closed doors, turned a corner, passing more as she made her way down. She would seek out the rear garden, the only place she seemed to find any peace at this interminable house party.

Moonlight spilled over the grounds, a rare, clear night. As Hélène moved to sit at her usual bench, she spied another figure already there.

Her immediate reaction was to flee. The ladies at the party were insufferable and she wasn't sure she could hold her tongue at the moment.

The figure turned. "Lady Gabriel?"

It was worse than Hélène supposed. Lady Michaella was the lone figure. She really could not bear to speak with the woman who still held her husband's heart.

Especially after what Mr. Wainwright told her just that morning. He'd discovered her reason for attending the party, the same reason he'd had for inviting them in the first place. She felt silly knowing he'd found her out but in her usual manner, she shrugged it off.

That didn't mean she had to speak with Lady Michaella.

"Please, Lady Gabriel. Hélène. May I speak with you?"

"My apologies, my lady," Hélène murmured, dipping a credible curtsy to her hostess, "I must... I am..." For the first time in her life, Hélène found herself at a loss for words.

"Please."

Hélène nodded. "*Oui*. Of course, ma'am."

"Call me Michaella, if you wish," Michaella offered, gesturing to the empty bit of bench beside her. When Hélène hesitated, she added, "I can understand your reticence, but I would appreciate the company."

Put so kindly, Hélène could not find it in her heart to deny the other woman. With an inward sigh, she lowered herself to the bench. "I fear I am not good company this night."

The moon shed enough light for Hélène to see Michaella's answering smile. "Then we shall be very well matched, I fear."

Settling her skirts round her, Hélène asked, "Then why request my company?"

"Have you never felt the need for human companionship with no desire to converse?"

Hélène couldn't help the smirk that tipped her lips. "*Oui*, on numerous occasions," she found herself saying before really considering how scandalous her words were. When Michaella simply nodded, she realized just how much innocence Michaella could claim.

Silence fell over them. Night sounds filtered to Hélène's ears. It soothed her. She felt a peace she'd not experienced since arriving in England at Gabriel's side some months prior.

"Do you still love him?"

Hélène felt the woman beside her turn. She could hardly believe the words slipped from her mouth but there they were, a living, breathing thing between them. She hated the way those words made her sound.

She chanced a glance Michaella's way. Michaella simply stared at her.

"I beg your pardon?"

"My husband. Do you still love him?" Hélène's tongue refused to stop, despite the disgust she felt at her own weakness. "Does he still love you?"

"I cannot answer for him," Michaella said, her tone low and gentle, "but my feelings are nothing more than those of a sister, I assure you."

There was no way to describe how those words made Hélène feel. It mattered not how Michaella felt, not really, but knowing she harbored no remaining romantic notions in regard to Gabriel brought Hélène a strong measure of comfort. Perhaps, given time, he would find that his feelings for Michaella were brotherly, rather than romantic, as well.

She rose. "*Merci*, Michaella. I am most appreciative."

Hélène strode away, her movements unhurried, contemplative. Michaella watched her leave, surprised to realize the truth of her own words. She sought merely to comfort her guest and in doing so, had managed to comfort herself. What had she worried over these past days?

Her immediate desire was to seek out her husband, assure him of her love for him, and beg his forgiveness. Then she recalled the inebriated state in which he'd presented himself not more than an hour hence and the desire to see him in that moment faded.

Shoulders slumping ever so slightly, Michaella sighed. There would be no conversation with Rhys this night.

Chapter Nine

Rhys woke with a splitting headache and a roiling in his middle that heralded a hellish day ahead. He groaned, rolling to his side. Rain streaked the window, adding to the dull, dreary sensation that filled his whole being.

How he wished he'd refused that last pint!

"Rhys?"

He stifled another groan before turning his head toward the door. "Michaella? Are you well?"

She moved closer, her brown hair drawn up and away from her unsmiling face. "I was about to ask you the same."

"What...what did I say...or do last night?"

Michaella grimaced, the expression so fleeting that Rhys almost missed it. "Nothing of import," she assured him.

He opened his mouth to argue, but noticed the set of her shoulders and the way her lips thinned as she stared at him.

She'd not say more on the subject and though he rather thought he deserved the peal she wanted to ring over him, he'd accept her ladylike restraint for the undeserved gift that it was.

He'd have to make it up to her, his lapse in gentlemanly behavior. He had some vague recollection of falling, Derringer's laughter ringing in his ears. Why had he ever accompanied those makebaits into the village?

"I will rise now." Michaella still stood there, as if she had something more to say but wasn't sure how to go about it. "If you are not planning to treat me to a well-deserved jaw-me-dead, my love, then perhaps you'd be so kind as to ring for my valet? I believe I will need his services this day."

Michaella hesitated. "I will not subject you to such an unladylike display." Her chin tipped up just a smidge, giving her features a rather adorably stubborn look. "Even if you do deserve it," she added under her breath.

Rhys grinned. "If you will not grant yourself the license to do so now, then I will make myself presentable for our guests and you can tell me your views on my behavior at a later time. Agreed?"

Her lips twitched, but she offered a solemn nod in capitulation. "Hart has asked after you. He wanted to be sure you survived. I will assure him you are well."

She swept from the room in the very best grand dame manner he'd ever beheld. As he levered his body up, firmly ignoring the pain in his head and controlling the upset in his stomach, Michaella returned.

She closed the door silently, leaning back against it while she worried her bottom lip. It seemed as though she had something to say but wasn't sure where to start or how to say it. Then, her lips firming, her wide eyes settled on Rhys. "There was a reason I came in here. Not merely that Hart asked after you." She paused as though needing to organize her thoughts. Then, "I do not know what has come over you, what made you go into the village and drink yourself senseless, but I love you." She paused just long enough to take a quick breath, adding, "And I long for the man you were before...before Gabe returned."

She was gone again before he could respond.

Chapter Ten

Michaella strode away, determined to lose herself in making her guests comfortable and forgetting the very personal thing she'd just blurted out to her husband. Why she'd felt the need to make that particular declaration on this morning, of all mornings, was a mystery.

And of all the things to say! As if he needed any confirmation that her odd behavior of late was directly related to Lord Gabriel St. Clair.

Michaella determinedly set aside her humiliation and made her way to the nursery. She wanted to see her sister, the one person who managed to calm her emotions when they threatened to take over.

A smile tipped her lips as she pushed open the nursery door. It was the opposite at one time. When they were children, it was Michaella who calmed the storms, especially the ones between Lady Harwood and Leandra.

Children played quietly in one corner of the vast nursery, two maids mending children's petticoats while the little ones played at their feet. On a settee sat Leandra, Penelope on one side of her while another little girl sat on the other. Two of the older children sat at her feet on the floor, listening with rapt attention as she read a story aloud.

After the scare Leandra had, the midwife suggested she take care in her daily activities. Leandra, terrified of losing her child, did just as the midwife suggested, but fretted over not being able to see her daughter daily. At Michaella's insistence, Leandra and her husband took up residence in the unused schoolroom. The servants moved a bed in and all the accoutrements a duchess could want or need and the Derringers settled in just as if it was the most natural thing in the world to reside in a schoolroom. Leandra was able to take her exercise in the spacious chamber, and she was right next door to the nursery, where all the children slept with their nannies and nursery maids.

Michaella was glad to see her sister looking well, and at ease. It was frightening to Michaella, the thought of her sister losing another child. She could only imagine how terrified Leandra must be.

She stepped forward to speak with the duke, who sat off to one side of the room with a newspaper and coffee, pretending as if he wasn't watching his wife like an overprotective nanny goat. It was sweet, Michaella thought, that the duke worried so over his wife. It wasn't something many husbands would even consider doing, at least not so blatantly.

Deep down, Michaella hoped Rhys felt enough love for her that he would worry over her during a time when many women, and their newly born babes, died. She'd seen noblemen simply shrug off the death of a wife, hire a nurse for the motherless child, and remarry after the requisite year of mourning if the child wasn't the anticipated heir.

She stopped by the little table. The duke glanced away from Leandra long enough to acknowledge her presence with a curt nod. He didn't rise, as good manners said he should, but Michaella would have been more surprised had he done so.

Still, she couldn't resist saying, "What a bad example you set, my lord. Those young gentlemen over there are watching you and see that you do not rise while a lady is standing. How will their nannies explain your behavior?"

He grunted, slanting a glance towards the young boys in question. Then, standing, he said, "You probably do deserve the honor. And I wouldn't want to be the cause of anymore bad behavior from those particular two."

His comment was directed at Michaella's niece and nephew, the two children who happened to be sitting at Leandra's feet. It was a rare moment of peace with those two, who spent their every waking moment wreaking as much havoc as they could without alerting their grandmother, Lady Harwood.

Michaella smiled as she sat in the chair opposite him. She said nothing as he stood there, staring at her. When he finally sat, she leaned forward. "Did that hurt? Was it painful to show good manners?"

He grinned. "No, not at all. But judging from the thunderous expression on Wainwright's face, I think you might find the next several minutes painful."

She whipped her head around. Rhys was indeed there, having entered the room without her knowledge. He caught sight of her and strode forward. She rose, her palms damp with nerves. What had her husband in such a pother?

Her words to him as she left his chamber? Heavens! She'd been most disrespectful and he was well within his rights to feel put out. She'd never before behaved with such a lack of decorum. Except once. When she'd first met Rhys and flirted with him though she was engaged to another man.

From the corner of her eye, she saw Derringer smirk. Then Leandra rose and the duke rose as well. Only for his wife did he show the proper respect.

But Michaella was out of time. Rhys bowed stiffly before her. "Madam, a word, if you please."

It was phrased as a question but Michaella heard it for what it was. An order, plain and simple. She excused herself to the duke and her sister, the latter of whom was nearly glaring at Rhys, and followed him out, matching her strides to his more halting gait.

Where he led her was not apparent at first. He said nothing, simply walking and expecting her to follow. Had he been anyone else, she'd have simply walked the other direction. She had her stubborn streak too, after all, and though she'd always been a good daughter, her father had never been one to snap out orders as if he were a general. Perhaps Rhys' days in his majesty's armed forces made him more likely to order others about, though he'd not shown such tendencies in the time Michaella had known him.

And that was the real reason she followed back down to the floor where the sleeping chambers were, her eyes firmly on his broad shoulders, the sound of her satin skirts swishing and his cane clicking in her ears as they moved. He'd never ordered her about before and curiosity over his actions now prompted her ready capitulation.

As they passed the room housing Gabriel and Hélène, that door opened. Michaella opened her mouth to greet Hélène as they passed, but Rhys didn't even pause. He marched on, as a soldier on campaign. Michaella paused regardless and offered the other woman a smile.

"Good morning, my lady. I trust you slept well."

Hélène grinned, a very cat in the creampot type of smile that almost made Michaella blush. "*Très bien*, Michaella," the Frenchwoman affirmed. She glanced past Michaella to Rhys, who'd stopped just down the corridor, awaiting his wife's return to his side. "Monsieur Rhys awaits you. I am not sure you wish to keep him waiting long, no?" She leaned closer, her next words clearly not meant to carry to anyone's ears but Michaella's. "He seems most...determined...to have you to himself."

Finding little to say in response to that personal aside, she simply nodded and excused herself. As she stepped away, Hélène added, "Please call me Hélène. We are to be *amis*, friends, you and I." She closed her door and sashayed on down the corridor, as if she hadn't just managed to completely shock her hostess.

"Madam?"

Michaella turned back toward her husband. He stood before her chamber, waiting for her. As she approached, he opened the door and ushered her in. She entered, confused, though it was clear he wanted privacy for whatever he had to say.

She turned slowly, just in time to witness Rhys locking the door. "Oh dear," she murmured, eyes wide. "Will you beat me? You do not want my sister, her husband, or the servants to come to my aid?" She knew what she suggested was absurd, but some small, melodramatic portion of her mind seemed to have taken over.

He frowned but said nothing. He simply stared for the longest moment, then he closed the distance between, each thunk of his cane upon the floor letting her know that if she didn't move soon, he'd be upon her.

She held her ground. If he was angry enough to beat her...well, that was something she'd have to contend with.

If he didn't, then what drove him now?

He raised his hand. Michaella didn't flinch, though it took everything in her to resist the urge. While she'd never believe he'd beat her, she also acknowledged that she'd known him less than a twelvemonth and how much could one learn about the true nature of a man, especially when he was angered, in that small amount of time?

He touched her, a fleeting brush of his fingers over her cheek. His hand curled over her cheek, and he drew her closer, pressing his lips to hers with a gentle insistence that told her better than any words that it wasn't simply anger that ate at him. His other hand curled around her ribs, pulling her closer. The soft thud of his cane hitting the carpet barely registered on her consciousness.

Things were getting out of hand. She now knew he wouldn't beat her, but clearly some discussion was warranted.

Reaching up, she pulled his hand away, already feeling flutters in her belly, heralding the incipient loss of her wits at any moment. Months into their marriage and she couldn't help what he made her feel, that quivering anticipation of his touch, of his complete and utter absorption in her, in them, what they did, and that sense that one was exactly where one belonged.

Her breath caught on her recollections, and the temptation to succumb was nearly overpowering. But she held tight to his hand. "What has made you so angry that you sought me out in the nursery in your condition?"

His lips twitched, reminding her of the man she'd married. "You make me sound as if I am a doddering old man at death's door. I have a sore head from too much drink. I'm not dying." He turned his hand, giving hers a little squeeze. "I am not angry, though I wanted to throttle you for walking out after what you said. Was I not entitled to respond?"

Her face warmed under his scrutiny. "Perhaps I did not care to hear your response. It was most unladylike of me and not at all as a proper wife should behave."

His smile turned to a full-blown grin. "My darling, we have discussed this very subject before. Did I not assure you then that a *proper* wife is something I'd not know how to live with? Was there something in my manner that suggested otherwise?"

"This house party was a mistake," she said, pulling away. "What possessed me to think it would be anything else?"

"This house party was exactly what you needed," her husband countered. "For weeks before your friends and family arrived, you moved about this house in a listless manner, taking little joy in activities you'd once enjoyed. I hoped family, friends, someone—anyone!—could bring you out of your melancholy."

"I have not been melancholy!"

Her voice rose in volume, loud enough to render Rhys

silent. He straightened, the slightest stumble reminded Michaella that he'd dropped his cane. She stooped to retrieve it, her skirts billowing out around her. She glance up from her crouched position, handing his cane to him.

"I apologize for that outburst, sir. It was wrong—"

He reached for his cane but grabbed her arm instead, jerking her to her feet none-too-gently. "Enough!" Michaella's brows rose at his vehemence. "I am done explaining there is no need for this. I love you. You, you fool woman! It doesn't matter what you say or how you say it. I will not beat you—yes, I noticed your fear—and I trust that your heart does not belong to another man. Stop apologizing!"

She smiled. Grinned, really. Her feet moved a step closer. "What if I was very rude? Does that not require some form of apology?"

He should have smiled but he didn't. His stern expression slowly killed her own smile and she tensed, attempting to step away. He refused to allow her retreat.

"Let us speak of the real reason we are here, now, when we should be in the dining room with those guests who choose to break their fast together, rather than taking chocolate and toast in their rooms."

"What reason is that?"

"You love me. You don't love Lord Gabriel St. Clair. While that certainly fills me with relief, I should probably tell you that I knew that."

She had nothing to say, but questions swirled through her mind. If he knew, why was he so angry? Why did his behavior these past weeks resemble that of a jealous man, rather than a man secure in his wife's fidelity?

"I'd begun to think you doubted yourself." He paused, glancing away from her for the briefest moment, as if he looked somewhere deep inside. When his eyes again met hers, they held a certain sadness. "It is a devastating thing, to doubt oneself."

She hadn't doubted herself. But she hadn't doubted him either. Now, in the bright light of day, in the arms of her husband, she couldn't recall what fear had caused her own aberrant actions.

Unable to find the right words, she did the next best thing. She closed the last few inches of distance between them and pulled his head down to hers.

Chapter Eleven

Hélène didn't know why, but her feet took her to the nursery. As each interminable day of the house party passed, more and more of the guests gathered there, being entertained by the children's antics or taking an opportunity to entertain the children. Her inability to successfully carry a child of her own was a constant gnaw in her middle, a failing in her as a woman that she felt unable to overcome.

She'd lost yet another one. Just after being welcomed into Gabriel's noble family, she lost the one she'd had no idea she'd managed to conceive. No more conceptions had occurred since but that was no surprise. Until the night just passed, she'd refused Gabriel his husbandly rights.

Many husbands would beat their wives for doing such a thing, but Gabriel had refrained. Though Hélène sensed his confusion, even his anger, she could not bring herself to welcome him into her bed, not with the knowledge that she'd lose another child. She just couldn't take it anymore.

Last night was...a mistake. After speaking with Michaella, she'd wanted to see Gabriel, determine if his feelings for his former love were as brotherly as that lady's feelings for him.

She'd forgotten just how affectionate her husband could be while in his cups. Or how much she desired him, despite the stupidity of her doing so.

She shook her head, her hand on the nursery door latch. She still couldn't fathom why she wanted to enter there. She'd not even had tea, nothing to settle the nerves in her stomach. She should have eaten something. Anything.

The door opened. The Duke of Derringer stood on the threshold, staring down at her with a questioning lift of his dark brows.

Hélène stared back. One would think she'd have gotten used to how much this man resembled her husband but there were still the briefest of moments that her heart skipped a beat. Then she would see the hardness of his eyes, the length of his hair, the thin scar marring his sun-darkened features, or that he clearly had two arms, and her heart would settle once again. Often, he merely had to speak, his voice lacking the incipient laughter that one could hear in Gabriel's voice.

"May I pass?"

There it was. "*Oui*," Hélène smirked, her momentary distraction broken. "As to your capability, I cannot speak. If you are like most nobles, you will need your valet, your butler, and several other servants to manage."

He grinned, as he always did when she teased him about his social status. "I'll see if I can do this on my own, shall I?" Before she could protest, he grasped her about the waist and lifted her out of his way. He spun, placing her inside the room. With a mocking bow, he disappeared.

Hélène shook her head and turned to face those in the room. More than just the children stared. But of the adults, the duke's wife was the only stare she looked for. Leandra's apologetic smile was unexpected and appreciated.

The more Hélène got to know Derringer, the more she realized he was no more a "noble" than she herself. He did the pretty when absolutely necessary and that was all. His wife was tolerant of his rebellious nature and very understanding when another was dragged into his sphere.

"Hélène, please join us."

Leandra's voice snapped Hélène from her brown study. "Thank you," she murmured, though her sudden desire to flee was nearly overwhelming. The duchess was very large with child and her precious young daughter sat beside her, reveling in the attention her mother gave her. The amount of jealousy that pierced Hélène was unbearable. Dark, hot, ugly, and red, alternating between the desire to weep and the desire to scream.

How she despised her broken womb!

She lowered herself to sit on Penelope's other side, the

little girl offered her a gap-toothed grin and snuggled closer. Hélène's eyes stung at the innocent gesture. The temptation to nudge the child away and leave the room grew. But some strange part of her mind, some odd desire to punish herself, made her sit right there and smile at the child, just as if she found the child's new dolly as fascinating as Penelope did.

"Beautiful, *chéri*," Hélène told Penelope, smiling at the girl's delighted grin. Penelope was satisfied with all the attention she'd received and slid from the settee. She toddled off to play with a little boy, one belonging to the Windhavens, if Hélène remembered correctly.

Leandra smiled at her daughter, then turned that beatific expression on Hélène. "Children are such a joy."

Hélène managed a smile despite the sinking in her stomach. "Indeed."

Leandra patted her hand. "It will happen. Have faith."

"Faith?" Hélène blurted. "Will faith overcome the loss of five babies in three years?"

Leandra's face paled. "Five? Oh, my dear, I am so sorry."

Hélène waved her concern away. "It is no matter. I have solved the matter. There will be no more babies to lose."

"But how?" Leandra's face burned, but she didn't apologize for her highly improper question.

Hélène studied her companion, brows raised. "There are ways, my lady," was all she'd say. The duchess didn't need to know that Hélène would not make use of any of those methods, nor would she reveal that the one she'd chosen to employ was the one most displeasing to her husband.

Leandra's face burned. As though sensing she'd wandered into forbidden conversational territory, she asked, "How are you enjoying the countryside, Hélène? Have you seen the village? I am told there is a beautiful Norman church but I have yet to see it."

Hélène's smile was sincere. "I have not, though I have no desire to do so."

Leandra laughed. "That was candid. Many say they wish to because one must to be polite, though they feel as you do."

"Thus I am impolite?"

"No, of course not," Leandra hastened to assure her. She leaned closer and lowered her voice. "To be candid myself, I've often wondered why lying is considered polite."

The children decided they needed the ladies' attention then, and Hélène found herself swept up right along with them, just as if she could lay claim to one of the little angels there.

Chapter Twelve

Gabriel wasn't really one for imbibing too much despite having lived for several years in a tavern. In his younger days, he'd not had much time for such nonsense, having enlisted at an early age to escape the man he'd believed to be his father. On the rare occasions he took the opportunity, he didn't suffer the following day as most others did. A mild pain in his head was all he had to contend with.

That and the memories of the previous night, the foggy, hazy recollections of his wife giving in to his seduction. What happened last night that finally brought her back to his bed, into his arms?

He also wasn't one to dally in bed all morning, at least not alone. He rose late, however, and found his wife gone. No doubt she was in the nursery again, playing with the babies and talking to the mothers who spent time there.

He wondered if she was increasing again. She'd lost

another one, maybe more. He suspected she no longer told him when it happened. He'd once been able to determine when she had, since she often avoided lovemaking for a time after. But it was months that she managed to avoid him this time, until last night.

What happened last night? He vaguely remembered her entering the room, sliding into the bed with him and kissing him. It was the strangest thing, really. He'd not been much in his sane mind at the time, still under the influence of strong spirits as he was. But he'd sensed a certain ease in her embrace, a certain...relief. He didn't understand it then and wasn't in any condition to try. He merely took what she offered and instead of turning away as she'd been in the habit of doing, she'd reciprocated.

He poked his head into the nursery. No one lingered there except the nursery maids who watched over their sleeping charges. One looked up from the linens she folded and smiled. She dropped the linens and curtsied. "Milord?" The other two maids followed her example, three young female faces attentively awaiting his reason for being there.

He waved them off with a smile and departed. Hélène was about somewhere, surely. In all the years he'd known Hélène he'd never known the woman to run from her problems, yet she'd done nothing but run ever since they discovered exactly who he could claim as family.

His arm tingled, a deep, dull ache shooting through his shoulder. He hated the phantom pain that often flared when his emotions ran high. But there was nothing he could do, short of ending his life, to stop it. He had to endure it. And the memories that went with it.

Instead, he focused on finding his blasted wife. She didn't ride, so he knew he'd not find her in the stables. She didn't care much for many of the ladies at the house party, so he doubted he'd find her gossiping with them in whatever withdrawing room they'd chosen for the activity. She had no interest in needlework, her sewing skills leaning more toward more practical uses such as mending clothing, so she wouldn't be with the other ladies who preferred quiet activities to gossip. She played no instruments and found little joy in music, so the music room was unlikely too.

He stood there in the corridor, rubbing his aching shoulder. His eyes moved around, his mind recalling every place he'd seen her in the house. The nursery was his first assumption but she'd clearly not been there or already left. Where could she be now?

The dining room held a few late morning diners, none of whom were Hélène. He was forced to stay and converse, briefly, but when he finally wrested himself from that social situation, he was right back where he started.

"Do you seek your wife, my lord?"

Gabriel turned at the question, his eyes settling on the pretty girl standing before him. He judged her to be of marriageable age, the sister of Lady Windhaven. "Miss

Emerson," he greeted. He sketched a bow.

"Sir." She curtsied. "I saw my lady heading in the direction of the rear garden. She is often there, taking the air."

He wanted to ask her how she knew that but she curtsied and left him, allowing him to blurt out nothing more than a quick thank you. He shrugged and made his way to the rear garden.

He'd never been one for greenery, but he could see the appeal of the garden as soon as he set foot in it. A wild tangle of vines and shrubs, flowers blooming here and there to add just a splash of color, with a single stone bench in the center would be just the thing his unorthodox wife would enjoy.

And yet, she wasn't there. Instead, he found Michaella.

Time slowed. She turned, no doubt hearing his step on the stone walk. He stared, his eyes remembering every aspect of her face, every look she'd ever given him, every moment they'd ever shared. He felt everything, all over again.

He'd feared this very thing. He feared seeing her again, truly seeing her, would rekindle all those old emotions, every single thing he'd felt for the innocent beauty before him. And he did.

But there was a difference. He felt those emotions, the tenderness, the protectiveness, and the joy, but that was all. There was no yearning to be with her, no sense that he'd come home, finally. There was only the pleasure in seeing a dearly loved friend, something he'd never considered having with a lady.

"Michaella," he greeted, stopping there on the path. If she approached him, it was her choice. But he'd not inflict his presence on her if she didn't wish it.

"Gabe." The word was a mere breath of sound, accompanied by a smile. She rose and took a step forward. Then she too stopped, merely staring.

"Come now," he said, laughing lightly, "one would fear our friendship did not survive my death."

"Oh no," she disagreed, her fingers tightening where they gripped her pale yellow skirts. "One would fear so much more than that." She took another step. "I must apologize to you, sir, for your reception here. I was not...gracious. I—"

He closed the distance between them and took her arm. "No. It is I who must apologize to you. I should not have inflicted my presence on you. It was insensitive. Cruel."

"Why would you think such?" Her brows knit above her honey-gold eyes. "I am beyond joyed to see you well and happy. I find your wife a true delight."

He was thunderstruck. "Why have we spent the past weeks avoiding each other's company?"

Her smile bloomed. "Fear?"

"Of...?"

"That our feelings had not changed."

She put the fear right out there, in the open. They were both married to others, trying to make lives for themselves without each other. And succeeding quite happily.

But always lurking just beneath the surface was the fear that their feelings for each other hadn't died, as they'd supposed, merely lain dormant until they were together again.

What a relief to realize it was not true!

Gabriel released a laugh that made Michaella jump. She stared and then laughed herself. He couldn't prevent the relief from spilling forth and he grabbed her round the waist, pulling her close. She wrapped her arms about him and squeezed him back, the joy apparent on her face as well.

"That's not something one likes to see in one's own home."

Michaella jumped back. Rhys stood behind Gabriel, brows raised but face expressionless. Hélène stood at his side, her stunned features blanking into a mask of Gallic indifference as soon as Gabriel met her eyes.

"Hélène!" Gabriel exclaimed, smiling. "I have been searching for you, love."

"And you found me in Lady Michaella's arms?"

He frowned. "No. What—"

"No matter. I am leaving."

She spun on her heel. Gabriel reached her side just in time to catch her hand. "What the devil does that mean?"

"You have found your love, I will leave."

Gabriel cast a quick glance over his shoulder. Michaella and Rhys spoke in lowered voices, heads close together. Neither one appeared upset. It appeared they could discuss their issues rationally.

Clearly, neither one was French.

"Even now, you cannot stop staring!" She launched into some gutter French she reserved for the moments her upset could not be properly explained in English. Gabriel allowed her to finish her tirade, forming his own arguments in his head as he waited.

He never got the chance. A servant hustled outside, her steps taking her to the stables. As she passed, she slowed only long enough to shout, "The baby comes!" before running flat-out to the stables.

Chapter Thirteen

"The baby!" Michaella dropped Rhys' arm and flew past, snagging Hélène's arm as she moved. The other woman didn't balk. They ran as fast as they could, skirts lifted high above their ankles to prevent the possibility of tripping.

The morning rain had cleared, offering a watery bit of sun that now disappeared. Dark clouds rolled back in and Michaella prayed it wasn't a sign that all was not well.

Leandra would be in a panic, with Derringer threatening bodily harm to the midwife and anyone else should they fail to successfully deliver the child and preserve his wife's life as well. Childbirth was dangerous and Michaella had to make sure her sister had the best possible chance of surviving.

She wasn't sure why she'd grabbed Hélène, but when the other woman didn't even hesitate, she was glad she did.

Childbirth was women's work and the more women who could help, the better, in Michaella's opinion.

She flew through the French doors and into the library, into the corridor beyond and up the stairs to the nursery. All the children had been moved elsewhere. The silence in the nursery was unnerving but not as unnerving as the muffled screams coming from the schoolroom that Leandra now used as her bedchamber.

Michaella burst through the door, Hélène hard on her heels. Leandra lay in the middle of the big bed, hair and face streaked with sweat, her once white nightrail stained with blood. Two maids were there, helping her as best they could.

Rushing to her side, Michaella took her sister's hand. Leandra forced a small smile, her breathing strained against the pain. "Kaylee!" The greeting ended on a high note as another wave of pain crashed over Leandra. Michaella winced as Leandra nearly crushed her hand.

Michaella turned her head. "Hélène, please see what is keeping the midwife. And get Lady Windhaven and Lady Greville. They have more experience with this than you or I."

"We are here!" Ladies Windhaven and Greville strode purposefully into the room, white aprons over their fashionable morning gowns and sleeves rolled back to reveal pale, slender arms. "We are here," Aurora, Lady Greville repeated. She positioned herself at Leandra's feet while Raven, Lady Windhaven moved to Leandra's side.

Hélène backed away. "I will find the midwife!" She was gone a second later.

Michaella stepped back, allowing the more experienced ladies take over.

"She will die."

Michaella turned at the horrified whisper. Derringer stared at his wife as she labored to deliver their child, his face unnaturally pale in the meager afternoon light streaming through the window.

Michaella took his hand, forcing his taut fingers apart. "She will not die. And you must not be in here now. You must leave."

"No!"

His harsh reply startled her and she dropped his hand. She pondered what to say to make him leave, but knew there was nothing to say. It didn't matter. He had to go. Leandra was struggling not to frighten him and she needed to focus all her energy on delivering a healthy child into the world. She could not worry over the feelings of her husband.

Michaella strode to the door. It opened as she approached, revealing Hélène and the midwife. She nodded to both and would have continued on her way had not Hélène stopped her with a hand on her arm.

"Where do you go?"

Michaella tipped her head at the darkly silent duke. "I

must get Gabriel to remove his brother. Hart will not leave and Leandra needs him to leave. She cannot do what she needs to do with him looking on, terrified she will die."

Hélène nodded. "Go to her. I will fetch Gabriel. Her grace needs you here, with her."

Michaella searched Hélène's face, detecting an odd note of panic and a touch of envy. She had no time to ponder that thought, however, and merely nodded, returning to Leandra's side.

Chapter Fourteen

Hélène sped through the manor, seeking the drawing room where she was sure she'd find the other guests, the gentlemen in particular. Part of her was relieved she could absent herself from the room where the duchess labored, a natural fear of the unknown taking over. But part of her longed to be there, to help bring the child into the world. She longed for her own child so much that she would even settle for being there when another woman had one.

The drawing room was full, every guest there waiting to hear news of the duchess. It was strange, and Hélène suspected many would find other activities to occupy them once they realized just how long it could take to birth a child. But for now, they spoke in lowered voices as they waited for news.

Hélène ignored everyone, striding to Gabriel's side. "Gabriel, we have need of you." Rhys stood next to her husband. She paused for a brief moment, then said to that gentleman, "You should come as well. It might take both of you."

"Let me guess," Gabriel murmured as the gentlemen followed Hélène from the room, "my brother is there and refuses to leave?"

"Please be quick." She stopped talking, taking the lead and refusing to acknowledge the feelings coursing through her. Anger, shame, jealousy, and sadness warred for dominance. None of them deserved her attention and certainly not in that particular moment. And unfortunately, as angry as she was, she still desired the cur. He showed his preference for another woman despite his protestations of love for her, his wife, and she still wanted his touch? What ailed her?

She shook her head at her own ridiculously weak feminine brain and strode quickly across the nursery floor to open the door to the schoolroom on the other side. The gentlemen strode right into the chamber, neither one sparing a glance for the laboring duchess in the bed. They marched over to Derringer, each man taking an arm, and marched his protesting self right out the door. Hélène stood back and marveled at this, not having deduced exactly how the men would manage to remove the stubborn duke.

As he passed by, Gabriel gave her a look she didn't understand. It was not the time for personal discussions, however, and she pushed the door shut with a soft click.

Fifteen hours later, Hélène swore she'd drop dead of exhaustion at any moment. Leandra labored silently on, her screams having faded into tired huffs as more and more blood left her body. Hélène feared for her life and the life of her child. The baby had to come soon or they would both die. They might both die anyway.

They layered more sheets under the duchess. Her hair was soaked with sweat and they'd changed her nightgown twice already. Hélène took her turn holding the poor woman's hand and for the first time, there in that darkened room as Leandra pushed with the last of her strength, Hélène was content to live the rest of her days without ever going through the same. While she still hated the fact that she conceived but was unable to successfully carry the child, she was content with the cards fate had dealt her.

But she couldn't be sure Gabriel sincerely agreed, despite his claims otherwise. A man needed an heir.

A scream ripped from the duchess' throat. Hélène tensed as her fingers were ground together so tight that the bones threatened to break. She ignored the pain and leaned close, whispering words of comfort in her native tongue, allowing the soft French to calm her and the soon-to-be mother.

All the women in the room were tired, worn to a shade, but labored on right beside Leandra. The midwife's furrowed brow instilled no confidence in Hélène, and judging by the expressions on the other ladies' faces, they felt the same.

"Let me," Michaella murmured, taking Leandra's hand and allowing Hélène to reclaim her bruised fingers.

Hélène moved to assist the midwife. She was grateful for the respite but at the same time, hesitant to assist in the part of childbirth she little understood.

"Too much blood," the portly woman muttered, brow furrowing even more. Then, all of a sudden, a tiny bundle burst forth, all pink and red. The midwife smiled and blew out a relieved breath as she gave the baby a smack on her bottom, eliciting an angry wail. She handed the child to Hélène with barely a glance in Hélène's direction, who held her tight as the midwife cut the cord that still attached her to her mother.

Hélène smiled, feeling an odd sense of triumph that had nothing to do with her. The little girl in her arms wriggled about, still protesting as Hélène determinedly wiped her tiny body with a damp cloth and wrapped her tight in a clean blanket. She moved to the bed, thinking to hand the child over to her mother. But the duchess screamed again, a short, shocked burst of sound that made all the ladies jump.

"Here comes t'other one!" the midwife announced, leaning back in to catch the next small bundle the duchess pushed from her overworked body. This time, the baby screamed out her rage, not even needing the midwife's customary slap. The cord was duly clipped and the newborn handed to Michaella.

Hélène stared with wide eyes. "Twins?"

Michaella's expression was no less astounded. "Twins."

Leandra laughed, a weak, breathless sound that was nearly swallowed in the rain drumming on the window pane. "Of course." She drifted off, too tired to even give her babies a look.

The other ladies shared concerned glances. The birth was hard, as was often the case with twins. The midwife worked steadily on, taking care of the afterbirth and cleaning the duchess up, all while the duchess slept the sleep of the exhausted. Her even breathing gave Hélène some comfort, though, even if the birth was harder than she'd expected.

"No," the midwife grumbled.

Hélène leaned close, careful to keep the baby in her arms close. "What is it?"

"Her grace bleeds too much," the older woman explained. She shoved more cloths between Leandra's legs in an effort to stem the flow. The midwife kept shaking her head, her lips drooping more and more with each passing second.

Pain lanced through Hélène. With the loss of each child she'd so briefly carried, she'd learned a few things about slowing the flow of blood afterward.

Stooping close to Mrs. Smythe, she whispered, "Mix ginger and cayenne with the bayberry. It will slow the bleeding much faster."

The midwife glanced at Hélène, giving her a long, searching look before nodding. "Quite right, milady. Should have thought of it myself." She gestured to a hovering maid and began issuing instructions with all the confidence of a general. Hélène stepped back, feeling a small measure of comfort that her own misfortune could benefit another.

Michaella moved in close to Hélène. "Hart will return. I do not believe Rhys and Gabriel can keep him away any longer."

"He cannot see her like this," Hélène breathed, feeling a bit panicked on the duke's behalf. "But what can we do?"

Lady Greville, her blond hair mussed and falling about her face in charming disarray, stepped up as she wiped her hands on a blood stained cloth. "Take the babies to Hart. He will be distracted enough to stay away until we can make her more presentable."

Hélène glanced at Michaella. "Will it work, do you think?"

Michaella shrugged, her eyes going to the mewling bundle in her arms. "It is worth trying, I would think."

Chapter Fifteen

Part of Gabriel was relieved he had never experienced the hell he witnessed his brother experiencing now. Derringer instilled dread in those he met, yet now, while his wife labored to bring his child into the world, the man wore the dread on his own face. It was a sobering thought.

The drawing room was empty of guests, early morning not conducive to socializing. It was a rare moment of peace, one Gabriel would have enjoyed more had it not been tinged with worry. He cared for Leandra, but it was Derringer's anxiety that really spoke to him.

"This is not right," the duke grumbled. His eyes strayed to the mantel clock. "Should it not be over by now?"

"I have no children, Hart," Gabriel reminded him. "I do not know. How long was her lying-in with Penelope?"

"I wasn't there."

Rhys placed a glass before the duke. He said nothing as

he poured a mouthful of brandy into the bottom. The duke quaffed it without question.

"Then we wait," Rhys suggested.

On his final word, the door opened. Michaella and Hélène walked in, each carrying something. As they approached, they smiled at Derringer. "Duke, meet your daughters."

The duke was on his feet and reaching out for Michaella's bundle before Gabriel even blinked. He and Rhys followed behind. Gabriel found the whole situation rather surreal. Derringer took one of his daughters and moved over to the window, where some meager light seeped through the drenching rain outside.

Gabriel moved toward Hélène, smiling at her wondering expression.

"Is she not the most beautiful thing, *chéri*?" Hélène asked. She opened the blanket enough so Gabriel could see. He smiled despite the very disloyal thought that the child was red and wrinkled and nothing remotely resembling beautiful that he could see.

He glanced at Hélène's face, saw the radiance in her features as she held another woman's baby, and realized that she was the most beautiful thing. How he wished he could give her this, but it seemed children were not in their future.

Her face lost its glow as she raised her eyes to his. "The birth was difficult," she revealed, her gaze sliding to where

Michaella and Derringer stood admiring the other baby. "Leandra was not conscious when we left the room."

"Will she live?"

"I do not know."

"Where's my other girl?" Derringer asked, sidling up close. Hélène jumped, not having realized the duke had managed to move without her knowledge.

At the sight of the duke's empty arms, Hélène glanced behind him, noticing he'd left the other baby with Michaella and Rhys. She turned fully, offering up the child she held. "Another beauty, your grace."

Derringer frowned at Hélène, but when he turned his gaze to his child, he was all smiles. He took the babe and cuddled her close. His words, however, were all for Hélène.

"Does my wife live?"

"Yes, my lord."

He glanced at Hélène. "Why the sudden formality? Did we not discuss that we are family and formality is wasted on the likes of me?"

Hélène smiled grimly. "Good manners are wasted on you as well, Duke."

He flashed her a grin before he strode away, talking to his newborn daughter as he went.

Gabriel's eyes followed his brother. Hélène caught the wistful look he tried to hide. Guilt stabbed her, even as she told herself she wanted no part of the pain and terror involved in bearing children. She felt like putting a hand against the dull ache in her middle, attempting to hold back the suffocating tears threatening to undo her.

Before her husband could turn and see the emotion she couldn't hide, Hélène fled the room.

Chapter Sixteen

Derringer, being Derringer, did not stay from his wife's side for long. As Hélène entered the schoolroom, she heard a commotion in the nursery behind her. Turning, she beheld the duke bearing down on her, determination in every movement of his tall form.

"My lord!" she exclaimed, placing herself between him and the bed. "Hart! Please, wait!"

"Let me pass."

The silky tone sent a shiver down Hélène's spine but she held her ground, putting one hand flat against his chest in an attempt to emphasize her unwillingness to let him in. His anxiety shivered through her arm, sending her own mind into a state of near panic, the uncanny reaction making her tremble. But she couldn't let him see his wife, especially if the duchess was dead, and at the moment Hélène didn't know. She firmed her resolve, remembering full well that the Duke of Derringer felt no compunctions about removing obstacles from his path—even if that obstacle happened to be a woman.

"You may let him pass, Hélène." Raven, Lady Windhaven put her hands into her lower back, wincing as she tried to ease the ache. She shot a smile Hélène's way. "Leandra is sleeping, but she is well."

Hélène breathed a sigh of relief and stepped aside just in time. The duke looked ready to mow her down, proper treatment of women be damned.

The midwife had left, all signs of childbirth removed from the chamber. The duchess lay peacefully in the large bed, her hair tidied and her breathing even. Near the bed was a cradle, just big enough for two small babies. It lay empty at the moment, the babies having been left in the care of their two uncles and their Aunt Michaella.

Hélène stepped up beside Raven and Aurora, watching the duke as he settled himself on the bed beside his wife. He slid his arm under her head, drawing her into his arms, and kissed her brow. His encouraging whispers of praise filtered to the ladies' ears. They heaved a collective sigh and left the duke with Leandra.

Raven and Aurora were worn to a shade. They took their leave of Hélène and withdrew to their respective chambers, intent on a few hours of rest before the day's activities commenced. Hélène, despite having toiled right along with the other ladies, found herself oddly restless. She went to her chamber to change, secure in the thought that Gabriel wouldn't be there. He would be too occupied getting to know his newest nieces, reveling in the joy of a new baby, even if that baby wasn't his own.

And he would want to stay in the riveting presence of Lady Michaella.

She ached at the thought, but determinedly hardened her heart. Tugging at her gown, she cursed the tapes that refused to come undone. Lady Michaella was boring, pedantic, a pathetic creature with more hair than wit. Hélène didn't know why any gentleman would love her, unless he wanted an empty, brainless peahen to bear children and be an ornament.

Except she wasn't, Hélène admitted as the sound of tearing fabric filled the silence. Michaella was none of those things, and if she had any flaws at all it was that she was too patient, too forgiving, too willing to believe the best of everyone.

But she could bear children. Even now, Lady Michaella carried a child, something she'd told the ladies while they helped Leandra Derringer bring her children into the world. Her fear had communicated itself to the ladies and they hastened to assure her that all would be well when her time came.

A single tear slid down Hélène's cheek. She swiped it away. She'd told herself at the time that she was glad she would never know the fear of a woman birthing a child.

And deep down, she knew she lied. She wanted a child, had always wanted children, and one experience witnessing a woman give birth, and a difficult birth at that, was not enough to change that desire.

With a frustrated scream, she ripped her green muslin gown the rest of the way, stepping out of it and throwing it across the room. It landed on a chair, or half on a chair, rather, a forlorn testament to her agitated mood.

Standing in nothing but her stays and chemise, her hands clenched. Anger was an emotion she was used to, one she knew rather intimately, in fact, but it would do no good. She had a decision to make. Would she stay with Gabriel knowing he loved another, or would she go, allowing him to seek a divorce and remarry?

Of course, divorce was entirely dependent on the English courts, but as the brother of a duke, surely one would be granted to Lord Gabriel St. Clair.

Hélène turned, her eyes still fixed on her feet. The light streaming in through the window flickered over her necklace, the silly little bauble Gabriel bought her all those years ago. She touched it, her fingers just barely brushing over it. Blue glass, the color of her eyes, and a pearl that was no doubt filled with wax, as was often the case when one couldn't afford a real one. Worthless to most, it was the most valuable thing she had. And she would keep it, as a reminder of the only man she'd ever loved.

"Do you require assistance?"

She spun about. Gabriel stood there, leaning against the door she'd failed to hear open or close. "Assistance?"

"You appear to be undressing," he observed, stepping toward her with the stealthy gait of a cat. "And the state of your gown would imply you are having difficulties. I thought it polite to offer my help."

Her hands went up in a defensive gesture. He stopped, his expression curious. "Don't," she whispered. "Just...don't."

"What did I do?"

"If you touch me, I can't...please don't."

"Hélène, what has come over you? You rushed off to help Leandra, vexed with me for what you believe to be an infidelity." He paused, studying her expression as if trying to glean her deepest thoughts. "Am I wrong?"

Hélène studied his face, unsure what to make of his odd calm. "I do not believe you to be unfaithful. That is not something you would ever be, my lord." He flinched at the formality, but made no reply. "I do not understand why you lied about your feelings for her."

"I did no such thing."

Hélène just stared at him, hands on her hips and completely uncaring that she stood there mostly unclothed. "That is all you have to say?"

Gabriel threw his hand up. "What else can I say?" He stalked closer, ignoring the fact that she took a defensive step back. "I have told you I do not love her, that it is you I love. What more can I say?"

Anger slid through her. "You embraced her! If you do not love her, why would you embrace her?"

Gabriel's lips twitched. "Darling, you know as well as I that love doesn't need to enter into an embrace."

She struck out at him, her fist connecting with his chest. He grasped her wrist and pulled her close. With a quick movement, he released her wrist and snaked his arm around her, trapping her against his chest.

Hélène fumed, but found his hold unbreakable. Part of her relished the closeness, but the other part wanted nothing more than to do him bodily harm. She settled for glaring at his waistcoated chest.

"Look at me," he commanded. When she finally, reluctantly, glanced up, he said, "I do not love Lady Michaella."

"But you did once."

"Yes, and we are not the same people we were all those years ago."

Hélène frowned, trying not to notice that his body was pressed intimately to hers. "What about you is so different?" Her gaze slid away from his face, focusing instead on the steady pulse of his heartbeat at his throat.

"You."

Her chin snapped up. "Me?"

"Yes, you." He paused, the slightest of smiles touching his lips. "And Rhys Wainwright." He dropped a kiss on her lips, refusing to be seduced when she sought to prolong the touch. She scowled, for some reason unwilling to allow him to speak. Though the last thing she wanted was seduction, there was some part of her that did not want to hear what he would say.

"You will not distract me," Gabriel assured her, smiling, a hint of laughter in his tone. "I changed when I met you. I may not have remembered who I was or where I came from, but I knew you. You accepted me despite my infirmity, despite my inability to be of much help to you or your tavern. You forgave me when I blundered, even when those blunders meant spending a handful of blunt you couldn't spare." He studied her, giving her a little squeeze when she would have looked down, her discomfort with his praise rendering her unable to say a word in response. "You should have thrown me back in the sea, but you didn't. I will be forever grateful to you for that."

Gratitude? Her heart sank. "You love me because you are grateful to me for saving your life?"

"No. I love you because you are you." He kissed her forehead. "I cannot help but love you, your strength, your tenacity, your unwillingness to lay down and die." He kissed her lips again, this time paying proper tribute, flutters of anticipation racing down her spine. "I love you, woman."

"Even if—"

He kissed her again, stifling her query. Her hands slid up

over his shoulders, pulling him closer. His hand pressed into the small of her back, melding their forms as close as possible with the layers of clothing that separated their flesh. He eased her across the room, kissing her as if she was the only woman left on earth, as if he feared losing contact with her lips would allow her to disappear from his life.

When her legs bumped up against the bed, she gasped into his mouth. Her body felt over-sensitized, even the slightest breath of air over her bare shoulders sending tingles through her whole being.

He released her lips just long enough to say, "Even if a child is never ours."

She opened her mouth but no words came. Indeed, what could one say in the face of such a declaration?

"I love you, Hélène, not your womb or its ability to carry children. I never expected you to be my brood mare, delivering child after child until you're haggard as a fishwife."

His urgent tone shivered through her, settling in her middle and easing the ache she'd carried for so long.

"If we have a child, we do. If not..." He shrugged. "We still have each other."

It was all Hélène needed to hear. The thing that weighed most upon her mind, the thing that made her feel less of a woman, less of a wife, did not matter. She pulled him to her, kissing him for all she was worth. He pushed her down to the bed, his lips never leaving hers.

As her hands began pulling at his clothes, he leaned away, propped up on his one elbow. "Hélène?"

She paused, her fingers busily undoing his waistcoat buttons. "Hmm?"

"Is there nothing you wish to say to me?"

She glanced up, her hands tangled in his waistcoat. "Say?"

Gabriel grinned. "Will you make me beg?"

A slow, intimate smile curved her lips. "The temptation is there, I admit."

He tipped his head to the side. "Hélène."

She smiled. "I love you and only you, *chéri,* though you vex me greatly, and there are times I think you will drive me insane." Her smile faded. "Children are important to a man in your position."

"Perhaps," Gabriel allowed, "but if children are not in the cards for us, so be it."

She could not mistake his sincerity. And instead of lamenting her childless state a moment longer, she decided to embrace the love she'd been given.

And embrace him she did.

Chapter Seventeen

Rhys lay in his bed, alone, as he'd done for many of the nights of this interminable house party. He stared at the canopy, idly wondering why they possessed such a bed. It was most unnerving, feeling trapped within a cocoon of dark silk hangings. He'd never understood the fashion and since it had long since been abandoned, why had they not abandoned it as well?

The door opened. Body tensing, he waited, silent as death, not sure who to expect creeping about his chamber in the middle of the night.

He hoped for Michaella. After her sister safely delivered twin girls the previous evening, Michaella's attention had been taken up entirely with the little darlings. He understood her distraction, but he couldn't help but feel a certain sense of neglect at the loss of her attention. It was selfish, he knew, but he'd been mostly neglected since welcoming so many guests into their home.

"Rhys?"

The whisper slid over him, his tense muscles easing in relief. It was his wife, creeping about as if she has no right, no wish to disturb him. Little did she realize just how much her presence...*disturbed*...him. Her innocence made him smile.

The bed hangings parted, just a bit, enough to allow in a bit of light from the candle she placed upon the nightstand. She'd yet to determine his whereabouts in the huge bed, so he relieved her of that chore, at least.

His hand shot out, grasping her wrist and pulling her down beside him. She squealed in shock or fear, he couldn't tell which and quite frankly, didn't care. He had her alone, finally, truly alone.

"Rhys!"

Michaella struggled to sit up, her hands pushing at his chest. He wouldn't let her.

"My love," he murmured, pinning her beneath him with his leg, "you ought to know better than to enter a man's room"—his gaze swept over her shadowed form, his hand following the path his eyes blazed—"in nothing more than this garment you sleep in."

Her breathing hitched. "You are in a mood," she murmured, her hand catching his. "I am come to talk, nothing more."

"Darling, talking is not what I have in mind."

He kissed her, stealing what remained of her calm, good sense, at least for a moment. But she rallied, determined to speak with him, despite the flare of desire at his skilled touch.

"Rhys!" She shoved at his shoulders, her fingers digging into his muscles, steeling herself against the shivers of delight she felt at the touch of his lips on her bared shoulder.

He paused, candlelight dancing across his face. The curtain had not fallen closed when she fell into the bed, a circumstance she was thankful for at the moment.

"Darling?"

"I must explain."

Rhys pulled away, fully releasing her from his spell. "Explain? What do you think you have to explain?"

"My actions. You saw me in Lord Gabriel's arms. Should I not explain?"

Pulling further away, Rhys pushed himself up against the pillows behind him. His face fell into shadow. Michaella frowned, unsure at his complete withdrawal. She sat up, facing him, tugging her nightdress back up over her shoulder.

"Again, what is there to explain?" he asked, his tone so blank she could tell nothing of his current mood. He certainly seemed to have lost any hint of seduction he might have been feeling.

She settled deeper into the feather ticking. Sighing, she

offered, "I know you were vexed to find me in such a way, and I am deeply sorry for how it appeared."

"But not because it happened."

It wasn't a question. "Nothing untoward occurred," she said, cringing at the defensive tone she heard in her voice. "In all truth, my love, it was nothing more than embracing a friend one hasn't seen in many years. Nothing more." Rhys made no reply. Michaella sighed, twisting her hands into the skirt of her nightgown. "Gabriel was very important to me at one time and though that importance has undergone a change, I still value his friendship. Can you understand that?"

"I do."

When he added nothing more, Michaella released a frustrated growl. "Then why do you look at me so? Why do you look at me in a different manner than you have always done?"

A moment of tense silence passed. Michaella's fingers tightened to the point of pain, but she ignored that.

Rhys finally leaned forward, his beloved features again falling into the glow from the candle. "I realized something in that moment," he said, reaching out to grasp her numb fingers. "I always knew what a prize I'd won, even before you took me to task for deceiving you. In that moment, though I knew you'd never play me false with Lord Gabriel St. Clair, I also knew your happiness was worth any pain, any sacrifice. If you wanted him, I'd have moved heaven and earth to make sure you had him."

He shrugged, releasing her and leaning back into the shadows.

Michaella seethed. "What?"

"Did you not hear—"

"Oh, I heard you," she snapped, leaning forward until their noses almost touched, "I heard you quite clearly. If you thought I still pined for Gabriel, why did you attempt to seduce me now? One last roll in the hay, milord?"

"Michaella, I—"

"No! You will not speak! It is my turn!" She rocked back, drawing her feet up under her to sit up on her knees. "Why would you think that? Have I not proven to you that it is you I love, you who I want to be with? I married you! Do you think I take my vows so lightly?"

"My love, you agreed to an arranged marriage."

"I would have broken that for you!"

Shocked silence followed her outburst. Rhys hardly dared believe her words. It was a happy coincidence on her part that the man she'd fallen for turned out to be the very man she'd agreed to marry.

"You'd have broken a legally binding engagement in order to be with me?"

"Yes."

No hesitation, not one moment to consider how she'd answer. Unable to resist, he asked, "Then why are you so shocked that I might think you'd break your marriage in order to be with the man you loved first?"

"I...I...do not know." She fell silent, her body deflating as she realized the verbal trap she'd gotten herself into. "There is nothing I can say to prove my choice, is there?"

"No, but there is nothing preventing me from believing you despite all that."

It took her a moment to digest what he'd said. When she did, she launched herself forward, striking him with all the force she could muster. "You vexing man! How dare you tease me so!"

Rhys caught her arms. "View it from my side, love," he implored, infusing his tone with the very best whine he could. "You offer yourself up, ripe for teasing, and I am a mere man. How could I resist?"

She tried to jerk her arms free but he held fast, drawing her closer, stopping only when she leaned over him, his own strength the only thing keeping her from falling full-length atop him. He stared up into her face. The flickering candle shined just enough light in her eyes to reveal the simmering rage she felt at his actions.

How he loved this side of her, this saucy minx she revealed only to him! She wouldn't dare show such emotion in public. He fell ever more in love with her, amazed he'd had deeper to fall.

He let go.

The breath left her lungs in a whoosh. He gave her no opportunity to respond, or even catch her breath, continuing where they'd left off minutes before.

He rolled her to the side, allowing her a brief moment in which she blurted, "I am with child!"

Perhaps he should have reacted differently, but he couldn't help it. He laughed. "Of course you are, darling." He smoothed a hand over her cheek. "I knew it when you came to me a few nights ago. Too many things have changed about you."

"Changed?"

His hand skimmed over her breast. Heat climbed her cheeks, though she knew he couldn't possibly see her embarrassment. And just what, she wondered, was there to be embarrassed about?

"Very well. You knew, as you are far more conversant in these things than I am. Why did you not inform me that you knew?"

"I wasn't sure if *you* knew."

She had to allow that. It had taken her some time and one improper conversation with Leandra before she was sure. "But how did you know?"

"You forget, love, I was married once before. We never had children but that didn't mean she never conceived. She did, once. The child didn't survive, but I remember the changes in her all too well."

Michaella didn't know how to respond. There was a tone in his voice she didn't understand. He never spoke of his wife. He'd loved her, and she'd died.

"Rhys, do you still love her?" And there it was, her own bit of worry, a worry she'd not dared entertain until that moment.

He leaned in, kissing her until she didn't care about any of it anymore. She would have allowed him to continue kissing her, reveling in the feel of his hands sliding over her skin, but he paused, saying, "I loved her. But not now. And not the way I love you."

He didn't kiss her again as she expected him to do. He watched her, and what he could glean in the dim light of the guttering candle was a mystery to her. She felt the way his eyes swept over her face, as if looking for something.

"There is really no way to prove that," she finally murmured.

His fingers brushed down her cheek and over her lips. He kissed her and she felt his smile against her lips. "No, but I mean to use the rest of my life convincing you of that fact."

Epilogue

Seven months later...

When it came time for Michaella's lying-in, her sister wasn't there, having family obligations of her own to occupy her. She had no one to attend her, no familiar faces to calm her in such a trying time. Her husband was terrified, she was terrified, and they tried their best to keep each other from succumbing to madness.

Each passing day threatened to send her over the edge. She stared out the window, hands clenched so tight they whitened, pain shooting through her fingers. She didn't notice. Fear dominated all.

How she wished Leandra was there! Why did she not write sooner, begging her to be there? Why had she thought she could do it on her own, no one but the midwife attending her?

"This is too much."

The statement lingered in the air, desolation shivering on every word. Memories of Leandra's difficult birth assailed her. How would Rhys survive the loss of his wife and child, again?

That thought brought her to her feet, slowly, lumbering up until she stood reasonably upright. Hobbling to the bell pull, her large belly leading the way, she reached up to give it a good tug, but a scratch at the door stayed her hand.

"Enter."

The butler's stately visage appeared through the open door. "Visitors, madam. Lord and Lady Gabriel St. Clair."

Michaella felt faint with relief. She was not alone. Hélène would be there, sharing the anxiety of childbirth even if she had no personal experience to impart.

"Show them in, please," she ordered, breathless, fighting to stay conscious. She forced her swollen feet to walk in the direction of the chair she'd just vacated, stumbling as emotion crashed over her.

"Michaella!" Gabriel leapt forward just in time. His strong arm came under her, guiding her large form to the chair. She huffed her gratitude as Hélène waddled closer.

"Hélène!" Michaella breathed, eyes huge with wonder. "You are..." She couldn't bring herself to mention such an indelicate subject, though she herself suffered the same condition.

Hélène's smile brightened the room, going so far as to lighten Michaella's melancholy mood. "I am, finally, *Dieu d'éloge*. I have more weeks to go yet, unlike you, *chéri*." Her smile faded. "How do you fare?"

"The baby comes," Michaella revealed, terror coloring each word.

Hélène stepped closer, placing her hands on Michaella's belly without so much as a 'by-your-leave.' "So he does," she murmured, her soothing tone doing nothing to calm Michaella's upset. Hélène straightened, offering her arm to the other woman. "Come, *chéri*, let us help this baby into the world. He must meet his father, *non*?"

Hélène nodded to Gabriel, who grasped Michaella firmly and helped her to her feet. They escorted her to the family chambers two floors above, Hélène cursing under her breath at the ridiculousness of placing the family's rooms so far from the drawing room.

"Ooo!" Michaella stopped, tightness clenching her middle. She bent double, tensing against the pain, only staying on her feet due to Hélène's and Gabriel's steadying grip. She breathed through it, slowly, willing the panic away. No one mentioned the pain, though she should certainly have realized. Leandra's screams echoed in her memory. How she wished her sister was there!

"Calm, *chéri*," Hélène soothed, "we shall see you through this." She gestured to Gabriel, who nodded and released Michaella to Hélène's capable hands. They made their laborious way into Michaella's chamber while Gabriel escaped to who knew where.

"I wish I could escape with him," Michaella heard herself mutter.

"Hush, *chéri*. He will fetch the midwife, the estimable Mrs. Smythe, and before you know it, the babe will arrive. Calm is needed now."

Much to Michaella's surprise, Hélène embraced her, whispering, "I understand. Allow me to carry the fear for you."

Rhys paced the drawing room under Gabriel's watchful eye. He often paused, listening, as if he could hear anything from the bedchamber above.

Gabriel leaned back in his chair, his eyes darting from the glass in his hand to his agitated companion. "I realize sitting still is not possible," he mused, "but I cannot think pacing about in that manner is comfortable for you. Have a drink."

Rhys paused, his astonished eyes landing in Gabriel. "A drink?" He glanced at the mantle clock. "It's barely half gone eleven."

"Do you have a point?"

"Do you wish to turn into your brother?"

Gabriel laughed. "There are worse things I could turn

into." His eyes narrowed. "There is nothing you can do for her right now, save keeping your hands off of her in the future, and though I'm not suggesting you drink yourself into a stupor, you do need something to ease the tension I can feel all the way over here."

Rhys stared. "Indeed?"

Gabriel's nod was all the answer he got.

Feeling a little as though he had no choice, Rhys sat. His leg ached, something he didn't dare admit to the other man. Gabriel set aside his own glass, pouring a few swallows of brandy into Rhys'.

"I know how Derringer felt," Rhys muttered, quaffing the amber liquid. He refrained from choking on the fire that seared his throat. "One tells the father-to-be that he needs to remain calm, but with no understanding of the impossibility of such a feat."

Gabriel nodded. "I expect Derringer will be at my side when Hélène's time comes, telling me to keep my sanity while I imagine all sorts of hideous outcomes."

Rhys grinned. "Congratulations."

Gabriel muttered an obscenity that had Rhys' brows shooting up. He almost laughed, but didn't think it was wise in the face of the other man's clear upset.

"I am happy at the thought, but do you realize just how hard it is to keep the woman from overexerting herself?" He set his glass down and filled it, fuller than before, a certain panic to his movements that Rhys wondered at.

"She is a demon. She doesn't listen, goes her own way, refuses to believe this one will survive either."

"Perhaps she wishes to protect herself in the event that she does lose the child," Rhys suggested, feeling much calmer.

"Yes, of course she does. But that doesn't mean she shouldn't take her ease more often than usual."

Rhys shrugged. "Mayhap you should allow her some license in this. We cannot fathom just how frightening this must be."

"Can we not?"

"No, how can we? We sit in a room and wait for someone to inform us the child has safely arrived and the mother has survived the ordeal. Our fear of losing both cannot possibly compare to the fear they must entertain. And the pain." He shuddered. "I am no stranger to pain—" He glanced at Gabriel's shoulder where there should have been an arm. "—and neither are you, but we cannot imagine."

Gabriel saluted him with his glass, then downed the remaining brandy therein and set the glass aside. "So we sit and wait, hope for the best, and imbibe just enough to keep us sane." He held up the decanter. Rhys wordlessly held out his glass.

"Are you frightened?"

Hélène glanced up from the linens she folded. "Frightened?" She smiled at Mrs. Smythe as that woman took her leave of them, offering to inform the gentlemen of mother and child's survival.

"Of this." Michaella tipped her head in the baby's direction. The tiny child suckled away, content with her new lot in life.

Michaella's tired voice lacked the panic it had held earlier, something Hélène was relieved to hear.

"Children? I do not fear children." She smiled at Michaella who smiled back in perfect accord.

"You know that is not what I meant." Sleep clouded her words. She stifled a yawn, the tension in her face telling Hélène just how exhausted the other woman was after her exertions.

Hélène sighed, returning her full attention to helping the maids clean up the room before Rhys made his appearance. "I am fearful, I admit. But I see little point in dwelling upon that which I cannot change. When my times comes, I will do the best I can to birth this babe and survive along with him."

She glanced over at Michaella. Her closed eyes suggested sleep, something Michaella needed very much at the moment. Hélène turned away, doing her best to finish the last bit of tidying before Rhys arrived.

Just as Hélène determined there was nothing more she could do, Michaella spoke.

"You will survive," she murmured, smiling. "You are a survivor, Hélène."

Hélène felt unaccountable tears spring to her eyes. It was amazing to her that one such as Lady Michaella would deign to consider her a friend, and yet, that was what they'd become.

She smiled at the other woman, finally, deeply content with her life. "As are you, Mrs. Wainwright."

THE END

About the Author

Jaimey Grant, a pseudonym for Laura Miller, was born in Michigan in 1979. After a fun-filled childhood interlaced with moments of emotional trauma and an insatiable curiosity about the reasons people act the way they do, she became a writer.

Primarily a Regency romance author, Jaimey has also dabbled in fantasy. A comprehensive list of works and where to find them can be found on her website, www.jaimeygrant.com. There are more Regencies and fantasies in the works.

She currently lives in Michigan with her husband and two children.

To learn more about Jaimey and her work, visit any of the sites below.

Website: http://www.jaimeygrant.com
Blog: http://www.jaimeygrant.com/blog
Twitter: http://www.twitter.com/jaimeygrant
Facebook: http://www.facebook.com/jaimeygrantauthor
Email: jaimeygrant@yahoo.com